The Temple of Wisdom

The
Temple of Wisdom

By

Karin Alfelt Childs

Fountain Publishing

The Temple of Wisdom

Published by Fountain Publishing
P.O. Box 80011
Rochester, Michigan 48308-0011

Library of Congress catalog card number: 97-90720

Manufactured in the United States of America.

First Printing 1997.

Cover art by Daniel Eller of 7th Generation and Karen Elder

ISBN 0-9659164-0-5

Dedicated to Annica.
I like to think we worked on this together.

Chapter 1

Brandun paced anxiously outside the chambers of his uncle, King Eadric. He tried to push the fear out of his mind, but its power made his heart pound. Eadric had been ill for a long time, the illness becoming more and more serious. For weeks physicians had shuffled in and out, talking in hushed voices. Brandun had fiercely refused to believe rumors among the servants that the King was dying; but now he had been formally summoned to the royal chambers, and the solemn tone of the messenger had tightened his throat. His ability to deny the rumors was weakening.

The sound of footsteps ascending the winding staircase at the end of the corridor startled Brandun out of his thoughts. The daylight of early summer streamed in through large, arched windows. But beyond that, at the shadowed entrance to the corridor, a dark form appeared, which then strode forward and became his cousin, Kempe. At sixteen, Kempe was bigger and broader than thirteen-year-old Brandun. His body was muscular from intense training in riding and battle skills. His auburn hair hung thick and straight to his shoulders, and his angular face held its usual look of cool confidence.

1

Out of habit, Brandun ran his hand over his own dark brown curls. He wished he could smooth them flat, for he felt that curls made him look young. Brandun searched Kempe's eyes — the same blue-green as his own — for any trace of emotion. It was always hard to know what Kempe was feeling. Sometimes Brandun wondered if he felt anything at all. Was Kempe also afraid at being summoned to the king's chambers, or at the possibility of Eadric's death? Kempe's eyes told Brandun nothing.

Kempe's mother, Defena, entered the corridor, looking beautifully royal, as always. Her thick auburn braid fell to her waist over a green silk gown. Defena's bearing, like Kempe's, was cool and emotionless. The three of them stood silently and stared at the door to the king's chambers.

Finally the heavy, wooden door opened, and Ladroc, the king's trusted steward, looked out. Brandun swallowed. "King Eadric will see you now," the steward announced. Kempe and Defena both stepped through the door, their postures straight and formal, their faces serious. As Brandun reluctantly moved to follow, Ladroc placed a hand on his shoulder, and for a moment, their eyes met.

Ladroc's kind face, framed with a dark beard and gray streaked hair, was a welcome sight. Ladroc had lived in the castle for longer than Brandun had been alive. He had always been a comforting presence, firm but compassionate, a scholar who loved to study old manuscripts in his spare time. He delighted Kempe and Brandun with tales of their uncle's kingdom, and of the times before it was formed. But now in Ladroc's gray eyes Brandun saw pain, and the wet glint that comes before tears fall. Here was someone who would also miss Eadric.

Brandun took a deep breath and stepped into the room. His eyes were first drawn to the splendid, stained glass window set in the midst of one wall. It held a scene of rounded green mountains, with a brilliant sun above. High on one of the mountains rested a small square of bright gold. A border of brightly colored ovals, gleaming like gemstones, surrounded the entire scene. Afraid to look at Eadric's bed, Brandun let his eyes wander about the room. He glanced at the tapestries on the walls, the finely carved wooden chests and benches, the various weapons hanging on pegs. Finally he let his gaze rest on the royal bed, and took slow steps toward it.

The colorful linen curtains that hung around the bed were pulled back. Eadric's wife, Queen Aeldra, sat on a stool and held the king's hand, and Brandun was alarmed at her appearance. Her usually bright eyes were clouded with fatigue as she gazed at her husband. Her back was rounded, her body hunched over, as if she were giving up and submitting to what must happen.

Sunlight filtering through the stained glass window decorated the still form under the white linen sheet with ironic color. Brandun thought about this bed as he approached. He remembered sleeping in it, warm and safe between Eadric and Aeldra, after he came to them as a five-year-old boy. He had no memory of his mother. She had died two days after his birth. Brandun's father

3

and Kempe's father had died in battle on the same day, in the same hour. Both men were brothers of King Eadric.

Brandun couldn't remember his feelings about his father's death, eight long years ago. But he could remember the nights in this bed, resting his back against the warmth of Eadric's body, while Aeldra stroked his brown curls and kissed him, weeping quiet tears for the boy who had no parents. Her touch had warmed his whole being, for he had never felt the touch or kiss of his own mother, though he had been told she kissed him before she died.

Brandun reached the royal bed and held onto the bed post. His legs weakened when he saw how frail Eadric looked. The king's hair and beard had turned completely gray. Aeldra turned to Brandun. Her face was weary and streaked from crying, but she smiled and held out her hand. "Brandun," she whispered.

Eadric's eyes fluttered open. "Brandun?" he asked. "And Kempe?" Kempe had been standing at the side of the room with Defena, and came to the bed when he heard his name. Loosing his hand from Aeldra's, Eadric weakly reached for the hands of his nephews. "My nephews, and my sons. From the time that your fathers died, I've considered you my children, Aeldra and I having none of our own. And it is time, my sons. You must now journey to the Jahaziel Mountains and search for the Temple of Wisdom."

"But — neither of us is yet eighteen," Brandun protested, confused. Eadric had always said that Kempe was to search for the Temple when he was eighteen, to try and acquire the golden scepter — the sign of the one who would be the next king. If Kempe was unable to find it, Brandun would try when he was of age.

"Sire," Kempe began hoarsely, then cleared his throat. "You speak to both of us. But am I not supposed to journey there first, and Brandun only if I fail to return with the scepter?"

Eadric released his nephews' hands. "Ladroc," he called weakly, "bring my scepter." Aeldra stroked his hair anxiously and murmured for him to save his strength while Ladroc moved to an ornate wooden chest and unlocked it. From it he lifted a scarlet pillow, on which rested King Eadric's golden scepter. Brandun looked at the familiar carving of an eagle at the top, noticing with surprise that the eagle was crumbling. Gold dust lay scattered about on the scarlet cloth.

Eadric laid a hand on the scepter. "You see that my scepter is crumbling away. That is because I am dying. A new scepter must be brought to the kingdom of Haefen."

"You're too young to die," Brandun blurted out, his throat swelling with a sob.

Eadric eyed him tenderly. "I know, Brandun. I have not yet seen sixty years. But disease takes those of all ages, and my heart is severely weakened. There is not time to send Kempe, and then possibly send you. You must go together, to determine the next ruler as quickly as possible." The king's tone had grown urgent, and it strained him. He paused for breath, and continued weakly. "If I die with no established heir, anyone even distantly related to me can decide they have some right to the throne, and there may be trouble."

Brandun's head reeled. He tried to listen, but his spirit crumbled at the thought of Eadric dying. Blinking back his tears he asked, "What if you die before we return?"

Eadric reached a frail hand for Brandun's and clasped it. "Brandun," he said, his voice now surprisingly strong, "when love exists between people, death cannot separate them. God makes sure of it. Whatever happens, it will be all right. I have been privileged to act as your father when my brother could not. There is a bond between us too powerful to break."

Brandun nodded, wiping his eyes and nose with his velvet sleeve.

"And Kempe," said Eadric, releasing Brandun's hand and turning to his other nephew. "You have had your mother, so you have not had as much need of Aeldra and me, but you are the son of my other brother, and have lived in this castle as *my* son since his death. I love you, and have great pride in you."

Kempe's lower jaw quivered slightly, and he swallowed. Then he nodded solemnly.

"Defena," Eadric called quietly. Defena moved to the bed, where she stood in stiff silence, eyes staring straight ahead.

"My brother's wife," Eadric said sadly. "Much has stood between us for the past eight years. Have you truly forgiven me in your heart?"

Defena bowed her head and blinked back bitter tears.

Eadric continued. "Though I was given the scepter

at the Temple of Wisdom, I have still been a fool at times. Kempe," he said, addressing his nephew, "your father and I disagreed when hostile tribes were attacking from the west. He had his plan of defense, and I had mine. Because I was king, I insisted on mine. If I had been thinking from wisdom, I would have seen that he had more battle sense — he always did. My folly resulted in the death of both my brothers, and years of regretful agony for me." Eadric looked back at Defena, who lifted her head and met his gaze.

"My added anguish has been that it needn't have happened," she told him. "But I know you love your brothers, and regret your mistake."

Suddenly Eadric winced and put a hand to his chest. Brandun gasped and leaned toward his uncle. Aeldra put her own hand to the king's chest, her eyes troubled. But the pain passed. Eadric drew a rasping breath and slid his hand back down to his abdomen.

"I want to be alone with Aeldra now," he requested weakly, his face fatigued. "Brandun and Kempe, make ready for your journey. Then come to bid me good-bye, and I will tell you more about the Jahaziel Mountains and the Temple."

Tears of protest dripped onto Brandun's cheeks. "I can't — leave you," he stammered, holding tightly to the bed post.

Aeldra rose and took Brandun's face in her hands. She kissed his forehead, then looked into his face and said, "Go, now." Her voice was gentle, but firm.

Brandun staggered as he turned toward the door,

breathing in shallow sobs. He felt an arm across his shoulders and looked up to see Ladroc helping him to the door. Ladroc patted Brandun's shoulder as they walked, and Brandun reached up and clung to his hand until they came to the door. Then Ladroc released him into the corridor on his own.

Brandun managed to stumble to the stable, though his body felt as heavy and numb as iron. He made his way to the stall where a dapple gray horse stood, nostrils twitching in a whicker of pleasure at the sight of his master. "Sparke," said Brandun, rubbing the horse's velvety nose and coarse forehead. The horse seemed to sense he wasn't getting his master's full attention, and nudged Brandun's chest impatiently with his nose.

"No, I have no treat for you today," Brandun scolded absently, walking into the stall. He looked around in confusion, knowing he must get ready for his journey, but feeling he had lost all ability to think. Grabbing a currying brush, he set to work on Sparke's gray coat.

As Brandun brushed, he heard someone coming. Kempe strode into the stable, dry eyed and steady, and entered the stall of his own bay horse, Sherwynd. A servant followed, bringing Kempe's riding gear. Brandun listened to the thumping and jangling as Kempe dressed his horse for a long ride. Hot anger rose from Brandun's chest into his head. Kempe acted as if nothing were wrong! Didn't he care that Eadric might die?

When another servant brought riding gear for Sparke, Brandun tried to focus on the task of preparing his horse, but his movements were slow and awkward.

Finally, in frustration, he asked the servant to saddle Sparke— a simple skill he had been doing for years, and should have been able to do with his eyes closed.

Defena swept into the stables and over to Sherwynd's stall. "Kempe," she said urgently.

"Yes," Kempe responded, fitting the bridle over Sherwynd's head.

"You must do your utmost to find the Temple of Wisdom and become the heir." Brandun could see that her fists were clenched. If she knew he was in the stable, it did not seem to concern her.

"After all," Defena reasoned, "you are the eldest one. It would have made your father so proud."

Kempe kept working without speaking. Defena grabbed his arm. He stopped and looked at her. "If you are king," Defena said slowly and deliberately, though her voice trembled with emotion, "no one can give you orders that might send you to your death." They looked into each other's eyes for a moment.

"I will do my best," Kempe promised calmly, "for you, and for my father."

Defena threw her arms around her son. Kempe let her cling to him for a while, then gently detached her, saying he must continue with his preparations. Defena nodded, regaining her royal composure, and turned to leave. Gracefully, she swept out of the stable, her auburn braid whipping around as she turned, her dress billowing behind her. Wistfully, Brandun wondered what his own mother had looked like.

Soon more servants brought saddlebags filled with

food and changes of clothing. Two swords and two daggers were presented, freshly sharpened and polished to a shine. A servant wrapped an ornate belt around Brandun's waist, and into the sheath which hung from it on his left side he slid the blade of the gleaming sword. The dagger was placed into a smaller sheath on his right side.

Kempe came up behind Brandun and placed a hand on his shoulder. "Looks as if we and the horses are ready," he said. "Why don't we go back in." Brandun was surprised by this gesture, which seemed kind. Kempe didn't make a habit of showing his younger cousin affection. Brandun's anger at Kempe cooled a little, though it still smoldered dully in his chest.

As they approached the door of the castle keep, Brandun felt frantic, knowing it could be the last time he saw Eadric. What should he say? How could he tell Eadric how much he meant to him? Eadric seemed more a father to him than his real father, whom he couldn't even remember. And how could he possibly turn and leave the royal chambers? Brandun's breath came faster, and he felt close to panic. He grasped the hilt of his sword, searching for strength. It would be crazy to leave now. Why couldn't they wait to go on this quest? Would it really make such a difference and endanger the throne if they stayed on for a while?

I'll convince him to let us stay, Brandun thought. I'll *beg* him! He held his head up determinedly, and saw Ladroc coming out of the door to meet them.

Ladroc's face was drawn and grave. He stood wringing his hands for a moment, his head down, as if searching the ground for what to say. Brandun's panic returned.

"The king has died," Ladroc informed them.

Kempe solemnly bowed his head, but Brandun exploded.

"No!"

Grabbing sticks and stones he hurled them angrily into the dust. He drew his sword and with a cry of anguish heaved it toward the keep.

"Then there's nothing to live for!" he yelled fiercely. "I won't go on this idiotic quest!"

Ladroc reached out to comfort him, but was pushed away. "I won't go!" Brandun repeated with tears streaming down his cheeks.

"You must go, Brandun," said a soft voice.

Brandun turned and saw Queen Aeldra, pale as a ghost, leaning against the doorway as if to hold herself up.

"Eadric was anxious that you and Kempe go as soon as possible," she continued weakly. "He fears for the stability of the kingdom. He said that in the past an undetermined heir has resulted in much confusion and struggle. It — it was his dying wish, Brandun."

Brandun ran to Aeldra, and she folded him in her arms. He sobbed freely, his tears turning the shoulder of her gown dark. "I didn't say good-bye," he gasped. "He went too soon. Why wouldn't he let us stay?"

Aeldra sobbed also. "He didn't expect to die so soon. His heart simply stopped."

"Don't make me go now," Brandun begged.

Aeldra stroked his brown curls, wet with her own tears. "You and Kempe will stay for the burial tomorrow. Then you will go."

Chapter 2

Eadric's body, dressed in splendid garments of scarlet and gold, lay on a platform in the courtyard under the shade of a towering oak. The king's personal guard stood at attention by the body as scores of people came to look, to weep, and to pray.

Brandun felt no desire to approach the white, still figure that used to be his uncle. The very sight of the body agitated him. People approached to express their sorrow, but he barely heard them. He bowed stiffly to each one without looking at them. Finally he broke away and walked swiftly through the deserted castle gardens. He passed through rows of fruit trees, his chest aching with longing to be near Eadric, but not knowing how.

At the furthest edge of the vast garden, Brandun forced his way through the tall, thick hedge that stood against the outer wall of the castle grounds. He collapsed in the two foot space between the hedge and the wall, relieved to be alone. Clutching the thick summer grass and weeds, he cried until his body relaxed from fatigue, and he dozed.

Low, male voices and a jovial laugh jolted Brandun back to wakefulness. Not wanting to be discovered, he stealthily rolled up against the wall and froze into stillness. Who would be laughing on the day of King Eadric's burial? The voices and footsteps grew nearer, and though the men talked quietly, in the stillness Brandun could make out the words.

"King Bardaric?" said one voice lightly. "That's quite an aim, Father."

The other voice laughed softly. "But she's an eligible widow now," it responded. "One simply needs the proper charm."

"What about the Temple of Wisdom, and the scepter?" asked the first voice.

"An old, fanciful custom," scoffed the second voice. "Can anyone think it more practical to hand the kingdom to children rather than to an experienced lord, just because of some golden fairy wand? Besides, you *know* I am skilled in, shall we say, special methods of persuasion."

"Oh, yes," agreed the first voice merrily. "I know better than anyone."

The voices trailed off as the men passed. When he felt it was safe, Brandun took a deep breath and moved his stiff limbs. He knew the second voice to be that of Lord Bardaric, a friend of Eadric and Aeldra. The first voice must have been his son, Garwine. Feeling dazed and confused, Brandun wondered if he had understood the conversation correctly. He stood up and cautiously peered over the hedge. There was no one in sight. He trotted along the outside of the hedge, away from the direction the voices had gone, until he reached the stable area. He circled the stable, then walked briskly toward the courtyard, hoping he looked as though he had been visiting his horse. As he arrived in the courtyard, Brandun saw he would not be able to speak to Ladroc yet. Ladroc was supervising the wrapping of Eadric's body in fine white cloth. A white marble coffin lay ready on a cart, and all the people present were forming a procession to escort the late king to his tomb.

Brandun's mind reeled and swayed with the mournful weeping of Eadric's subjects as he walked solemnly with the procession. Aeldra rode in a litter suspended between two chestnut brown horses. Brandun walked beside one of the horses, and reached for Aeldra's hand over the horse's back. A cart drawn by two black horses rumbled over the dirt road ahead of them, carrying the coffin toward the burial ground which lay among gently rolling hills about a mile behind the castle. Nothing seemed real to Brandun; it was as if someone he didn't know lay in the smooth marble coffin.

The burial ground stretched between two rows of stately maple trees. Great slabs of stone covered each grave, carved with the name of the one buried as well as symbols that had adorned their family crests or scepters. Aeldra released Brandun's hand to slide off the litter. Ahead of them gaped a hole dug by servants earlier in the day. Four muscular members of the king's personal guard lifted the heavy coffin off the cart and lowered it onto ropes held taut by six servants. Aeldra walked to the freshly dug grave. Standing at the head of the coffin, she raised her arms skyward.

"Not dead, but passed on to greater realms," Aeldra

recited loudly, as was the custom at royal burials. She lowered her arms slowly, then added in a tender, quavering whisper, "God's peace to you, Eadric."

Six servants eased the coffin into the ground. As he watched it disappear, Brandun felt a surge of desperation rise in his throat, and he fought back a shout of protest. Stinging tears wet his eyes as the weeping of the people resumed. Brandun looked over at Defena and Kempe. Defena's face showed no expression. Kempe looked tired and pale.

Noblemen and noblewomen approached to embrace Aeldra. One handsome nobleman caught Brandun's eye with his confident stride and graceful manners. It was Lord Bardaric. Bardaric bowed his head of thick, honey-colored hair, streaked with distinguished gray, to kiss Aeldra's hand. Then, raising his face to look at hers, he gently wiped the tears from her cheeks with his fingers.

"You must go home, Aeldra," he said softly. "You need to rest."

With his arm around her shoulders, Bardaric led Aeldra back to her litter and gallantly helped her up. "See that you go slowly and give the queen a peaceful ride," he called to the servants who led the horses. He took Aeldra's hand and said softly, "Poor, sweet Aeldra. I will take care of you." Aeldra nodded numbly, but did not look up at him.

Brandun ran up beside one of the litter-bearing horses and grabbed Aeldra's other hand possessively. "I'll walk her back," he blurted out, blushing at his boldness toward Bardaric. Bardaric eyed him thoughtfully.

Brandun felt small in this nobleman's presence, and it was only a fierce protectiveness that kept him standing firm. After a moment, the corners of Bardaric's mouth turned up in a smirk of amusement.

"It seems your young nephew wants to play the part of escort," he said. "So be it for now. Later, when you need a man's care instead of a boy's, I will be at your service."

The horses started forward, and Brandun walked beside them. He fought to hide the anger at Bardaric that burned in his head, and wondered if his face was red. But when he looked at Aeldra, she was staring blankly ahead, not noticing him.

Brandun calmed himself and asked, "What are the greater realms, and what is God's peace?"

"I do not know," Aeldra answered, still staring ahead. "But I believe that both exist."

Back in the king's chambers, after the crowds had gone home, Brandun sat on a bench and stared numbly at the lustrous colored panes of window glass that formed the Jahaziel Mountains. Kempe sat across the room, leaning his elbows onto his knees and holding his face in his hands. Defena sat next to him, holding him with one arm and leaning her cheek on his shoulder.

"You are remembering your father's burial," she assumed tearfully.

Kempe heaved some shuddering sighs, but did not answer.

Aeldra lay on the royal canopy bed, her eyes closed in exhaustion. Kneeling by her side, Lord Bardaric held her hand and stroked her hair, murmuring soothing words. Brandun hoped that Ladroc would return soon. The steward was meeting with the carvers to discuss Eadric's gravestone.

Finally Ladroc quietly entered the room, and Brandun jumped up to meet him. "I must talk with you," he whispered urgently, grasping Ladroc's arm and leading him back out the door. They walked swiftly along the corridor to Brandun's bedchamber. Brandun sat down hard on his bed, pulling Ladroc with him in his urgency.

"Ho! Easy there!" exclaimed Ladroc. "What is it?"

Breathlessly, Brandun told what he had overheard at the edge of the castle garden. "Is he going to try and become King Bardaric? Can he do it?"

Ladroc's face had grown pale, and he lowered his eyebrows in anger.

"I have no trouble believing he'll try. He has told the servants he'll stay at the castle to care for Aeldra and her affairs until she is strong again. But it seems his concern is not for Aeldra. I gather his plan is to marry her."

"Aeldra won't marry him!" Brandun retorted hotly. "Look how much she grieves for Eadric! They were in love."

"Aeldra is greatly weakened by her grief," Ladroc pointed out, "and I'm afraid she might be easy prey for someone like Bardaric. She would never suspect a friend of trying to take advantage of her. He's very persuasive, and might convince her that she needs him."

"We've got to warn her!" exclaimed Brandun jumping up. Ladroc pulled him back down.

"Bardaric is a slimy creature under that gallant exterior," Ladroc said with contempt. "A friend among his servants has told me his lord's main purpose in life is to advance himself, and that he always manages to get what he wants. But anytime I tried to convey this to Eadric or Aeldra, they grew upset with me. To them, Bardaric had always been a loyal subject and charming friend. They said I had been listening to malicious gossip."

Brandun flopped onto his back in frustration. He knew if Aeldra hadn't been willing to hear the truth before, she'd be in no state to hear it now. And if Bardaric found out what they were trying to tell her, he might become dangerous.

"But he doesn't have the scepter from the Temple of Wisdom," Brandun argued, sitting up. "Nobody will accept him as king without that."

"Aeldra, being a woman, may only act as an interim ruler. This has always been the way. She will rule until the next male heir is able to take over the throne, but no heir is established yet. From what you heard, Bardaric thinks he can convince Aeldra and the people that he would be a better choice than you or Kempe, and that customs can be changed. That's just the kind of snake he is," Ladroc snarled, striking the mattress with his fist. "Never openly attacking, but slithering his way into people's trust until he has them under his control."

Ladroc tapped his fist on the bed in broody silence. Then he turned to Brandun and took him by the shoulders. "You and Kempe must leave on your quest immediately, without Bardaric's knowledge. If one of you rides back with the scepter before he has Aeldra in his coils, it will be clear who the heir to the throne should be."

Brandun hesitated. "Once an heir has been established, the only way to seize the throne would be to — kill that heir." He swallowed hard.

"But Bardaric would then risk being found out and severely punished," Ladroc reasoned. "Eadric has many friends who respect the sign of the scepter, and would protect the new heir."

Brandun had a sudden strong wish that he were a simple peasant. "Let's tell Kempe it's time to go," he said quietly, trembling at the responsibilities that might lie ahead.

Behind the stable, out of view of the castle keep, Brandun plucked at Sparke's gray mane nervously. His spirit was heavy with sadness and confusion, and he didn't like the uncertainty of the future. Would he become heir to the throne? Would Kempe? Would Bardaric gain the throne before they got back? Would someone try to kill the nephews of the king, to get them out of the way?

Kempe left the stable leading Sherwynd, saddled and ready to travel. Once again, he momentarily put a hand on Brandun's shoulder. "I'm sorry, Brandun," he said. "I know you'll miss Eadric."

Will you miss him? Brandun wanted to ask.

Defena and Ladroc came to see them off. They had not told Aeldra, for fear Bardaric might find out. "I want you far away before that snake knows you're gone," Ladroc told them. "A servant is making sure he will not see you pass through the gate."

Defena and Kempe both looked quizzically at Ladroc. "Why do you call him a snake?" Kempe asked. As Ladroc quickly explained Lord Bardaric's plans, Kempe's expression turned hard, and Defena's eyes grew wide with alarm.

"Do all that you can," Defena told Kempe, clinging to his hand, "as if your life depended on it! Honor the memory of your father."

Brandun's eyes met Ladroc's, and the king's steward smiled encouragingly at him. Kempe mounted his big bay horse and turned toward the gate. Beyond lay the road that led east. Brandun mounted and followed, leaving his home and his childhood behind.

Chapter 3

In the cool misty dawn, Brandun and Kempe rode slowly onward. After sleeping two nights on the ground, Brandun's stiff muscles ached. His stomach churned with hunger, but they had eaten the last of their hastily packed provisions the day before.

"How will we get more food?" Brandun called to Kempe, who rode in front.

"We'll stop at the first village or town and buy some," Kempe shouted back. Brandun wondered if Kempe felt as sore and hungry as he did. His older cousin held himself tall and confident, as if nothing could bother him. Brandun sighed quietly, hoping Kempe wouldn't turn around and see how tired he looked.

At the top of the next hill, Brandun was relieved to see a town about a half mile off. As if sensing his surge of hope, Sparke broke into a brisk trot.

"Food!" Brandun called out to Kempe as he passed him. "And maybe a comfortable place to rest a while!" Kempe urged his own horse into a trot and followed.

As they approached the houses that stood outside the town walls, all seemed strangely quiet. There were no people bustling about their morning business. Brandun and Kempe stopped their horses and looked around, puzzled. Kempe, seeing a bucket of water and a dipper near one of the houses, dismounted and helped himself to a drink. Just as Brandun was about to do the same, a woman shuffled out from the house. She walked like an old woman, though she wasn't old. Her faded dress was dirty, and her brown hair had been carelessly tied back with a frayed piece of cloth.

"Good day," said Kempe, grinning grandly. "My cousin and I are traveling and wonder if we could purchase some food and perhaps rest a while."

The woman walked slowly over to them, staring at their rich clothing. She looked up at them with tired eyes, and wearily brushed some hair from her forehead. "Most the town's in bed with fever. Hit us so fast we hardly knew what was happening."

Brandun and Kempe glanced at each other in alarm. Seeing their look, the woman was suddenly filled with desperate energy. She lunged for the reins of their horses, grabbing hold of them as Kempe swiftly climbed onto Sherwynd's back. "Please," she implored, "don't go. We need help. There are so few of us left to tend all the sick. I can give you herbs to strengthen you against the disease. I know much about their healing powers. The sickness came so quickly I didn't have time to set my mind to a remedy before most of the town was helpless in bed." She looked pleadingly at each boy's face, her knuckles white as she clutched the reins.

Kempe began to back up his mount. "I'm sorry," he told the woman, who was being pulled along by his horse. "I'm on important business for the kingdom. I can't stay."

"Please!" the woman begged. "These people are part of the kingdom! And I can teach you how to heal with herbs. It's a powerful knowledge!"

Kempe turned his horse so that the reins were torn from her hand. "I'm sorry," he repeated, "but I can't risk losing the time or my health."

The woman, still gripping the reins of Brandun's horse, let out a groan of despair.

"Wait. It's all right," Brandun told her, feeling awkward. "Let me go talk with him." The woman nodded silently and let go of the reins. She lowered herself wearily and sat on the ground as Brandun rode over to Kempe.

"We can't just leave her like this!" Brandun hissed.

"What can we do here but get sick and maybe die?" Kempe whispered back angrily.

"She said she could give us herbs to guard against the disease."

"What makes you so sure we can trust her miracle herbs?" said Kempe scornfully. "Besides, I was not meant to be a sick nurse! I'm the King's nephew, on an important quest. If we die here, what would become of the kingdom with no heir to the throne? No, a person must set his priorities and stick to them. I'm sorry these people are having a hard time, but I can't solve everyone's problems. Now let's leave. I don't like the feel of this place."

A moan from a nearby cottage sent shivers up

Brandun's spine. He grabbed Kempe's arm. "Listen," he said. "I don't want to stay here either. I don't know how to take care of sick people, and I don't want to get sick. But look at her." He glanced back at the woman sitting on the ground. "They need help!"

Kempe shook Brandun's hand off his arm. "Do as you like, little cousin. Come with me to search for the Temple of Wisdom and help the kingdom, or stay here and die!"

Kempe turned his horse toward the road. Brandun tried to grab Sherwynd's reins, but missed. "Kempe!" he said angrily. "Don't go! Helping part of the kingdom *is* helping the kingdom!"

But Kempe was already riding away. "Kempe!" Brandun screamed. "Don't leave me!" Panic seized his chest. He didn't want to be left alone in this place of disease. He didn't want Kempe to go on ahead and probably find the Temple of Wisdom long before him. He wanted to dig his heels into Sparke's sides and ride like the wind after his older cousin.

Instead he buried his face in Sparke's mane, feeling utterly alone. "I can't just leave!" he moaned. "It wouldn't be right!"

Brandun took some deep breaths and looked up at the tiny figure of Kempe disappearing in the distance. "Eadric would have wanted us to stay, Kempe," he whispered fiercely. Brandun jolted at the light touch of a hand on his leg. It was the woman.

"God bless you, young lord," she said earnestly. "You are brave and noble indeed. My name is Lufu."

Brandun slid off of Sparke and followed Lufu to her house. It was a tidy, wood-framed structure with a thatched roof and plaster walls made with twigs, straw, and clay. Inside, a small fire glowed in the middle of the only room, adding its light to the meager amount that passed through the tiny windows high on the walls. A simmering pot of water hung on a pole above the fire. On a straw mattress in the corner, two children lay restlessly next to a man who appeared to be sleeping.

"My family is sick," Lufu said. She pointed to a wooden bench. "Please sit down." Brandun sat on the sooty bench, while Lufu brought him four smooth, white cloves of garlic. "Garlic is the best defense against disease," she told him. "Eat them all." Brandun hesitated. He had never eaten plain garlic before. But Lufu stood watching, so he thrust them into his mouth and chewed. Suddenly his mouth and throat were on fire. He gagged and choked, and his eyes and nose watered. Lufu calmly handed him a dipper of water.

"Get it all down," she told him as he gulped the water desperately. "You'll need to eat garlic every day, but you'll get used to it." She went to a table where various herbs lay in piles. She picked out a few, eyed them carefully, and dropped them into the pot of heating water. "Our town is called Tamtun," she said, stirring the herbs. "We're a free town, not owned by any lord. About four hundred people live in and outside its walls, but I've found only thirty who have not been knocked down by the fever." Lufu smiled at him. "You see why I'm desperate enough to grab a kind young

25

nobleman who happens by. Who are you, and where are you going?"

Brandun let one more sip of water slide down his throat, which was now only mildly burning. "My name is Brandun."

Lufu furrowed her brow. "Tell me you're not Prince Brandun," she said.

"Well...I am."

"Heaven help me," Lufu exclaimed softly, leaning against the table. "I've gone and dragged a prince into my service, against his will!"

"It's all right," Brandun assured her. "I chose to stay. You won't be punished."

Lufu shook her head. "The truth is, I'm too tired to even care." Shuffling over to stir her brew, she paused to look Brandun in the face. "I'm deeply touched by the kindness of your heart. It's a true sign of greatness."

Brandun blushed and looked down at his lap. He didn't want to be here, and knew he didn't deserve such praise.

After the herbs had brewed, Lufu gave some of the mixture to her husband and children. "I must go on my rounds now," she told them, stroking each forehead.

"Mama, don't go!" whimpered the little girl, starting to cry. "I feel so sick."

"I know, my sweet thing," said Lufu soothingly. "And you're such a brave girl. You rest now with your father and brother, and I'll be back soon." The boy lying next to the girl looked as though he might cry too, but he kept his mouth bravely shut. The man gazed at his wife's face with eyes that glittered with fever.

Lufu poured the rest of the brew into two clay pots, and gave one to Brandun to carry. As they left the house, Lufu wiped her eyes with the back of her hand. "It's hard on a mother, to leave her family when they want so much for her to stay." She took a deep breath and straightened her shoulders. "At the first house," she told Brandun, "I'll show you what to do. Then we can tend to houses separately." Brandun followed her into the first house they came to. In the shaded light, a mother and three older boys lay on straw mattresses. Lufu knelt by the mother, lifted her head, and helped her drink a dipper full of the herbal brew.

"There," she said gently. "That will help." She took a cloth that lay draped over a bench and dipped it in a bowl of water next to the mattress. After squeezing it out, she gently bathed the mother's face and neck. "You rest now, and I'll check on you later."

The three boys kept having coughing spasms. Lufu gave them each a dipper of the brew. "Such coughing," she said sympathetically. "Perhaps a plaster on your chest would help. I'll see what I can do when I come again." She bathed each face and neck, speaking encouraging words. She took their water bowls outdoors to fill them from a bucket. "They need plenty of water," she told Brandun. "When the buckets become empty we fill them at the well in town or at the river down the hill." Leaving the freshly filled bowls by the mattresses, Lufu left the house, assuring the family that she would be back later.

"Now, Brandun," she said in a business-like tone.

"You will visit those five houses that we see to the west, and I will visit those six to our east. We will meet back at my house and then go into the town." Brandun watched in dismay as she walked away, then slowly turned and headed for the first of his houses.

Stepping inside he found an elderly man and woman lying on a mattress. The man sighed in misery, and the woman reached toward him. Reluctantly, he approached, and saw that their bowl of water had spilled. He looked at their parched, cracking lips. "It's all right," he told them, kneeling down. "I've something for you to drink." He was loath to feel the matted hair and the hot skin as he lifted the woman's head. Her eyes glittered, and her chest rasped with each breath. He shuddered, feeling as though he were touching the sickness itself. The woman drank greedily from the dipper of brew, and then lay back with a sigh of relief. After doing the same for the man, Brandun took the empty bowl outside and returned with fresh water.

As he dipped a cloth in the water, he pictured the loving carresses of Lufu's soothing hands. She didn't seem to mind touching her patients at all. She thought of them as people, not as sicknesses. *I chose to stay*, he thought. *I can choose to care.*

"This will feel good," Brandun told the man and woman, carefully wiping their hot, dry faces and necks with the wet cloth.

"You are a good boy," the woman whispered hoarsely. She closed her eyes and relaxed, and Brandun relaxed, too, with each wipe of the cloth.

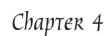

Chapter 4

All through Brandun's first and second day in Tamtun, he carried his pot of herbal brew from house to house. He walked through the narrow streets of the town, climbing steep stairs in the tall, thin houses to the living quarters above the empty shops. No one worked at their trades. The few people who were well enough to move about spent their time caring for the sick.

Brandun bathed many dry, hot faces, and spoke encouraging words. He walked again and again to the well in the quiet, market square to fill the household buckets with fresh drinking water. He helped Lufu and others scrounge up any food they could find for themselves and for the sick people who wanted to eat. Brandun milked cows, gathered eggs, and fed livestock whose owners were sick. He looked for bread or cheese stored in people's houses. The crops growing in waving fields outside of Tamtun were not yet ready for harvest, but Brandun found wild strawberries to bring home in a basket. When some of the men brought fresh meat, he helped cook it on spits over a fire, or boil it into stew in large cauldrons.

Amidst all the exhausting work, the hardest thing to

bear was death. Brandun kept his distance when the men sadly carried a limp figure out of the town to bury. "I hate death," he told Lufu when the elderly woman he had first taken care of was carried from her home, still and white.

Lufu, standing behind him, grasped his shoulders. "I know, Brandun," she said softly.

On the morning of his third day in Tamtun, Brandun rested in Lufu's home after his rounds. He drank a dipper full of brew, as Lufu had instructed him to do each day, and nibbled slowly at a clove of garlic. "It's not so bad if you eat a little at a time," he told Lufu. Lufu smiled wearily, bringing in a bucket of fresh water for her family.

She walked to the table, now only sparsely covered with a few herbs, and put her hands on her hips. "We've practically stripped every herb garden in town. Today we must go out to the fields and woods to find more. Let's tie some baskets and sacks onto your horse. We also need firewood."

Leading Sparke, Brandun followed Lufu away from Tamtun. "The herbs I know for reducing fever aren't working," Lufu told him. "I want to try some that might bring on a sweat and break the fever." Along the worn dirt road that passed by Tamtun, she stooped to pick a small plant with pink flowers, a hairy stem, and bluntly oval leaves. "Basil thyme," she said, holding the spicy smelling leaves to Brandun's nose.

"Shall I gather more?" Brandun asked.

"Yes, all you can find," Lufu answered, walking a

few steps further, "and lots of this Blessed Thistle, too." She carefully picked another hairy stemmed plant with yellow flowers and gingerly held it between her fingers. "Be careful of these," she said, pointing to the thin, cleft leaves covered with tiny spines. "They're sharp!"

They continued on through meadows that swayed in the summer breeze. Lufu pointed out a plant as tall as Brandun, with heart shaped leaves and clusters of purple flowers on top of round, hooked burrs. "Great Burdock. The root, once boiled, is good for bringing on sweat, and the leaves are good to eat." Brandun yanked at the large plant until it was torn from the ground, only to have it cling stubbornly to his clothing by its burrs. Lufu laughed and helped him pluck the plant from his tunic.

Down near the river that flowed past the north side of Tamtun, they approached the edge of a woods. Brandun kept his eye out for dead, fallen wood to gather for fires. There they found and gathered Devil's-bit plants with long, pointed leaves and thick roots, and Rocket plants with sweet smelling pink flowers. "Those flowers smell even more wonderful in the evening," Lufu said. "At night, their perfume fills the air."

"You know so much about plants!" Brandun exclaimed. "How did you learn it all?"

Lufu laughed. "From others who spent their lives studying them. I marvel at all God gives us in these growing things, and there is always more to learn. I will never know it all."

It was easy to laugh and talk with Lufu in the sunshine and breeze, away from the ominous sickness of

31

Tamtun. Lufu's affectionate ways suddenly reminded Brandun of Aeldra, jolting him with a pang of homesickness.

They returned to town with the baskets and sacks stuffed full of herbs and firewood. Lufu set to work immediately to prepare the new herbs into a brew, using the roots of some, and the leaves or flowers of others. Once the mixture had simmered long enough and then cooled, Brandun filled his clay bowl and set out. "Give them each a good, full dose," Lufu called after him as he went out the door.

That evening, Brandun collapsed onto the pile of straw covered with a woolen blanket which served as his bed. His body was heavy with fatigue, and his mind heavy with discouragement. All afternoon he had worked to care for the people to whom he had been assigned, and to give them ample portions of Lufu's new brew, but no one seemed any better. He gloomily wondered if they all would stay sick until each one finally died. In spite of the occasional whimperings from Lufu's children, he finally sank into an exhausted sleep.

In the first grayness of dawn, a cry of alarm startled Brandun awake. It was Lufu's daughter. "Mama! I'm all wet!"

Lufu hastily sat up and reached for the girl. "Her hair is drenched, and so are her clothes!" She felt the clothing of her son and husband. "Brandun! Their fevers have broken!" Brandun raised himself quickly and came to their mattress. Lufu hugged her husband's head to her chest, tears flowing off her cheeks and onto his wet hair.

"It's all right," Brandun told the bewildered children. "Your mother's crying because she's happy. You're getting well!"

Brandun was overjoyed to find that many others in the town had also awakened all wet. To those whose skins were still hot and dry, he gave another dose of the herbal brew, and words of encouragement filled with new hope. He ran and told the other caretakers in Tamtun about the broken fevers, and soon several more pots were bubbling with the new herbs.

The day was still filled with work from beginning to end, because even those whose fevers had broken were still weak and needed care. But Brandun's energy was revived, and he plowed through his duties with zestful vigor and cheerful conversation.

As evening descended over Tamtun, Brandun sat in Lufu's home, nibbling on a clove of garlic. Lufu's husband sat up on the mattress, talking about soon getting back to his summer haymaking. The children lay on their stomachs at the edge of the mattress, rolling marbles carved from wood. Lufu watched them with a wide, relaxed smile.

In spite of his happiness and relief, Brandun felt a nagging within that kept growing. "Lufu," he said. "I'm worried about Aeldra." He had told Lufu, bit by bit over the past four days, about Eadric's death, Bardaric's intentions, and his quest. "Every day that goes by could mean worse trouble for her. I have to at least know if Kempe found the Temple of Wisdom."

"Well," said Lufu softly. "I guess it's time for you to

go. Things will improve quickly now that the fever is on its way out." She reached over and took his hand. "I've never grown so fond of someone so fast. I will miss you, Brandun, and can never repay you for what you've done." Brandun felt his face flush and looked down at his lap. "But I can do something," Lufu continued, jumping up. "I know a woman whose youngest son outgrew his clothing a short while ago. I'll ask if you can have them. I'm afraid your fine clothes are contaminated, and should be burned. Wearing commoner clothing, though, will make you less noticeable if Lord Bardaric should decide to search for you and do you mischief."

In the morning, Brandun shed his stained and torn royal travelling clothes and put on a woolen homespun tunic and leggings. As he saddled Sparke, Lufu brought out two sacks. "Here is some cheese and bread and salted meat," she said, holding up one sack, "and this other sack has a few of each of the herbs we gathered, in case you feel yourself becoming sick. I've thrown in a few bulbs of garlic, too," she added, her eyes twinkling, "because I know how fond you are of chewing them."

Brandun smiled and secured the two sacks behind his saddle. He strapped on the belt that held his sheath and sword and turned toward Lufu. "Thank you," he said. "It was hard work being here, but — I'll miss you too." Lufu wrapped her arms around him in a quick, hard hug, then silently watched him mount. Sitting tall in his saddle, Brandun headed toward the road that led east.

The steady *clop-clop* of Sparke's hooves pounded along the worn dirt road for hours. Brandun passed an occasional traveler, but mostly his eyes and ears took in the waving, rustling fields of grass and the musical calls of birds. The river that had run by Tamtun stayed in his view, winding sometimes nearer to the road and sometimes farther, sparkling in the summer sunlight. In the late afternoon he saw a town in the distance to his north, but he knew Kempe would have headed steadily east to find the Jahaziel Mountains, so he stayed on the road.

Brandun felt lonely and unsure, traveling by himself. Thoughts of Eadric's death, which he had pushed away during his busy days at Tamtun, came flooding back. His mind numbly replayed the day of the funeral, denying what it all had meant. But once in a while panic seized his chest and he would cry, realizing he would never see his uncle again.

After eating some meat and cheese, Brandun spent the first night wrapped in his cloak in the tall meadow grasses. During the next two days, the road took him through a forested area. It was in the late afternoon of the third day since he had left Tamtun that Brandun saw in the distance a horse without a rider. The woods were thinning back into fields, and the horse grazed leisurely. It was a large bay horse, with a black mane and tail. Brandun's heartbeat quickened as he drew nearer because it looked like Sherwynd.

By the time Brandun reached the horse and hastily slid off Sparke's back, he had no doubt. He recognized Kempe's saddle and bags. Brandun looked wildly around, calling Kempe's name. He started through the grass toward the river, then broke into a run when he saw someone lying beside a rock near the river bank. The motionless figure lay with his eyes closed. The ornate, blue travelling clothes and the auburn hair were disheveled and stained with mud, but the figure was most definitely Kempe.

With his heart pounding, Brandun knelt down and placed his hands on Kempe's chest and throat. He felt the soft thumping of Kempe's heart echoing in the pulse in his neck, and laughed with relief. "Kempe," he said, taking his cousin's face in his hands.

Kempe's skin was hot and dry, and his lips were cracked. He drew in a rasping breath, and opened eyes that were glazed with fever. "Brandun," he whispered.

Chapter 5

"How long have you been here?" Brandun asked urgently, but Kempe closed his eyes and didn't answer. Brandun ran back to Sparke who was grazing beside Sherwynd, and rummaged in one of his bags. Quickly he seized a small wooden bowl used for drinking water and carried it to the river, where he thrust it under the flowing current. Scooping up the clear, cool water he brought it dripping to where Kempe lay and lifted his cousin's head to help him drink.

Kempe gulped desperately, then lay back with a sigh. Brandun rubbed his hands fretfully through his brown curls, trying to focus on his next step — treating Kempe with Lufu's herbs. He trembled to think that he might be Kempe's only hope for survival.

Leaping to his feet, Brandun again ran to his saddle bags and grabbed a handful of herbs. He tore two cloves from a garlic bulb and pushed them whole into his mouth, sucking on them while he thought.

I must have a fire. Brandun picked a spot five steps from Kempe and began to tear up the stubborn meadow grasses and flowers. When a circle had been cleared, he jogged into the edge of the woods and gathered an armful of dead branches. After building a crackling fire, he tossed into it many small stones from the river. While the stones heated, he filled the wooden bowl with water and a small portion of each herb. He knocked the scorching hot stones out of the fire with a stick, and dropped them quickly into the bowl. This heated the water enough to simmer the herbs, and Brandun prayed it was enough to release their healing properties.

For the rest of the day, Brandun made doses of herbal brew and gave them to Kempe, until finally he dropped exhausted next to his cousin and fell asleep.

As the light of morning first penetrated his eyelids, Brandun heard a sleepy voice close to his ear. "What have you done? Dunked me in the river?" Brandun bolted up and grinned with relief.

"Your fever's broken! You're going to be all right."

When Brandun had brought Kempe a drink, the older prince felt able to relate his story. "I think I fell sick about three days after leaving Tamtun," he began. "I had convinced a passing traveller to sell me some of his food, but after two days I started feeling strange. I finally stopped here, too dizzy to ride any more. For a while I could crawl to the river for water, but even that became impossible. If you hadn't come..."

"Do you feel like eating?" Brandun interrupted, holding out some bread. Kempe slowly chewed a few small bites, then handed it back.

Brandun helped Kempe out of his clothes and rinsed them in the river while Kempe sat wrapped in his cloak. For the next two days, they stayed there by the river, allowing Kempe's appetite and strength to return. On the third day, Kempe was still weak, but felt he could ride. "Our food is gone," he reasoned. "We must move on."

After half a day's travel, the weary cousins spotted a village just south of the road. They approached the large group of houses, built of wood and plaster with thatched roofs. Brandun could see flocks of sheep on small hills in the distance, and men in the fields surrounding the village, swinging their scythes through the thick grass near the river, while women raked it into piles to be stored as hay.

Brandun and Kempe rode slowly past the houses, looking to see if the village had a market square with food for sale. The people bustling about their morning business stopped to stare: a carpenter, sitting in front of his house, repairing a plough; a boy and girl, dropping grain to their chickens and gathering eggs; a woman, carrying a bucket of water and holding a small child by the hand.

Ahead, Brandun and Kempe saw a stone house much larger than the others, with fruit orchards on the left, and stables and barns on the right. The people leading cows from the barns out to pasture stared and whispered to each other. A slender girl near the stable caught Brandun's eye. She wore the tunic and leggings of a boy, and her long, straw-colored hair was braided down her back. Her stare was not one of curiosity, like the others. Her mouth hung open slightly, and her eyes were wide with amazement. Brandun looked her in the eye as they passed, and she did not turn away.

"Should we be careful not to tell who we are, and

where we're going?" Brandun asked Kempe as they stopped in front of the stone manor. Before Kempe could answer, the heavy wooden door of the manor swung open, and a lord in a richly embroidered robe and a gold neck chain emerged, followed by two attendants. The lord's hair and beard were jet black, and he looked familiar to Brandun.

"What have we here?" the lord asked, looking at them with intense interest.

Kempe hesitated, but then spoke evenly. "We are on a journey, and wish to purchase some food."

After eyeing them a moment, the lord broke into a wide smile. "Please come into my home. I would be honored to entertain you as my guests." He swung around and walked briskly back toward the house, while the attendants helped Kempe down and led his horse toward the stable. They did not help Brandun, but waited for him to dismount so they could take his horse as well. Brandun was surprised, until he realized that in the clothing Lufu had given him, he looked like a servant rather than a prince. He grinned and slid off Sparke's back, trotting to catch up with Kempe. Together, they entered the manor.

In the great hall of the manor, colorful carpets hung on the walls, along with the antlers of deer and other hunting trophies, and several shields and weapons. The stone floor was strewn with rushes, and bones from previous meals lay here and there, having been picked clean by dogs that now lay lazily on the floor.

The lord stepped up to the head table, which rested

on a dais. "Bring food to my guests!" he ordered loudly. While servants scrambled hastily to the kitchen, the lord motioned for Brandun and Kempe to be seated at the table. "I am Lord Thearl," he said with a wry grin. "I welcome the royal princes to my humble home."

Brandun stiffened, wondering how this lord knew who they were. "Yes," Lord Thearl continued amiably, but Brandun could sense triumph in his tone. "I attended the funeral of King Eadric not long ago. I saw your majesties there, but perhaps you did not notice me in the crowd. My heartfelt sympathy goes out to you both. I suppose you now search for the Temple of Wisdom?"

Brandun looked at Kempe, whose features remained unruffled. "What we are doing is not your affair," Kempe responded coolly. "We need to purchase some food and be on our way."

Thearl laughed. "I see you don't want to reveal the purpose of your journey. But I am a descendant of the great Daegmund, just as you two and Eadric are. I've made a point of learning all about my family history." He leaned forward and narrowed his eyes slightly. "The same blood can be coursing through all branches of a family tree, but fortune smiles more on one than the others."

"We're tired," Brandun blurted out, "and don't wish to talk. Only to eat."

A hint of annoyance flashed across Thearl's eyes, but then the dark haired lord smiled cordially. "Of course, your majesty. Forgive my senseless prattle." Thearl stood up and faced the kitchen. "Fools!" he yelled. "Must these men wait all day for a little food?" There were scuffling noises in the kitchen, and then three servants scrambled in with platters of beef, mutton, venison, strawberries, bread, and sweet pastries. They placed pewter plates in front of Kempe and Brandun, and filled pewter goblets with wine. Brandun dug in hungrily, but noticed that Kempe ate very little.

"Idiots," Thearl fumed as the servants retreated to the kitchen. "They simply won't do anything unless I scream at them. As for my villeins, their laziness resulted in poor crops last year, which brought little money to my coffers. That is how they repay me for the land and home I provide for them! If it goes the same this year, *they* will be the ones to pay." He regained his composure and smiled. "I'm sure your majesties are familiar with the challenges of maintaining order among those who work for you."

Brandun chewed heartily on a mouthful of bread; Kempe stared at his plate, looking paler by the minute.

Thearl stood up. "I will have a place prepared for you to rest and spend the night. We can talk more later." With a cordial smile, he turned and strode across the great hall, disappearing up a winding staircase.

"That man's a lunatic," Brandun whispered to Kempe. "Let's gather some of this food and leave."

Kempe let his head fall into his hands. "I have to rest," he said. "I can't ride now."

Brandun glanced around the room. Near every door, attendants were watching them closely. "All right," he said quietly. "You rest a while. I'll find our horses, and figure out when and how we can leave."

42

Brandun stood and addressed one of Thearl's attendants. "See to his need for rest," he ordered, pointing at Kempe. "I must groom my horse." He felt the glare of scrutinizing eyes as he walked out of the great hall and turned toward the stable.

What to do? Kempe was still weak. Thearl reeked of sinister thoughts. Would he stop them if they tried to leave? What did he want? Brandun rounded the corner of the stable, colliding with someone who cried out in surprise.

"Oh, I'm sorry!" the girl exclaimed. "You were so quiet walking up!" Once again, Brandun looked into the eyes of the girl he had seen earlier by the stable, but now he was close enough to see they were a beautiful, rich hazel. She seemed about his age; her skin was browned from the sun, and freckles lay sprinkled across the bridge of her nose and her high cheekbones.

"Who are you?" Brandun asked awkwardly, wanting to add: *Why were you staring at me like that?*

"I'm Larke," the girl said quickly, "the daughter of Marshal, who cares for Thearl's horses. I want very much to talk to you, because I — well, I saw you and your lord in a dream last night."

"My lord? Oh, you mean Kempe — he's not —what do you mean, in a dream?" Brandun stammered.

"Larke!" barked a voice that made Brandun jump. Lord Thearl swept past him, his face red with anger, and caught Larke by the arm, pulling her away. Thearl sucked in a deep breath through his nose to calm himself and addressed Brandun with forced tolerance.

43

"I thought your majesty had come to groom your horse, not to familiarize yourself with my villeins. I have chosen Larke to be my bride when she turns fifteen in the spring. I will not have her talking closely with young men who might try and draw her attention. I hope your majesty understands the importance of this."

Thearl turned to Larke. "Go back to your home," he ordered sharply. "Stay there for the rest of the day." Larke pulled her arm out of his grasp, rubbing it where he had held her. She looked once more at Brandun, then turned and ran toward the village houses.

Brandun's blood boiled at the rough treatment Thearl had displayed. That pretty young girl marry this lunatic lord? He clasped the hilt of his sword, feeling a tremendous urge to draw it and threaten Thearl. "That's no way to treat your bride," he murmured defiantly.

Thearl's countenance darkened. "The people in this village — the villeins — are my tenants. They are indebted to me for everything they have. It is my right to regulate them, and my right to arrange their marriages if I choose. I have chosen my bride, and she must begin learning to be a faithful wife."

Brandun heard Eadric's voice in his memory. *Don't be so hot headed,* he had told Brandun many times. *Lashing out is not the way to right the world's wrongs. It often brings more trouble than help. Think things through!*

Brandun took a deep breath as he met Thearl's dark stare. Three attendants had moved up behind their master, and stood ready for his orders. Brandun relaxed his hold on his sword and stated, "I will groom my horse now."

Thearl smiled slowly. "Very good. My attendants will stay, to assist you in any way you desire."

Chapter 6

As evening fell, Brandun sat fretfully on a wide bed in the room Thearl had provided. Kempe lay sleeping beside him, breathing in slow, easy rhythm. A tapping knock sounded on the door, and a thin, bald servant pushed his way into the room, carrying a pitcher of water and a bowl, and a feather quilt over his arm.

"For y-y-you," he stuttered, placing the pitcher and bowl on the ground and handing the quilt to Brandun. Brandun thanked him, noting how uneasy the servant looked. After closing the door, the servant knelt down and looked Brandun earnestly in the eyes.

"C-c-can't speak w-w-well," he whispered, his face contorting with effort as he struggled to form his words. "Th-th-thearl thinks I-I'm sssstupid. T-t-talks in ffffront of m-m-me. Thinks I w-w-won't t-t-tell, 'c-c-cause I'm sssstupid and afffraid to be b-b-beaten." The servant scrambled up to open the bedroom door and peer out, then returned, his eyes wide with fear.

"D-d-don't c-c-care this time. I-I'll t-t-tell. H-he w-w-wants to be k-k-king. Ffffollow you to T-t-temple of W-w-wisdom. T-t-take scepter and k-kk-kill you. Ssssay y-you had a-a-ccident — sh-show scepter to e-everyone

46

and ssssay h-he o-ought to be k-k-king." The servant grasped Brandun's shoulders, asking with his eyes if he had understood.

"Thearl wants to follow us, to find the Temple," Brandun repeated. "Then he'll take the scepter for himself, get us out of the way, and claim the throne. Is that it?"

The servant nodded vigorously. "I-I'll g-g-go now," he stuttered, lifting himself and moving nervously toward the door.

"Thank you," Brandun called out softly, realizing full well how brave an action this had been.

The servant nodded at Brandun, the fear leaving his eyes for just a moment, then slid out through the doorway and was gone.

In the great hall the next morning, Lord Thearl sat with Brandun and Kempe, sharing bread and ale. "Will you be off today?" he asked cheerfully.

"Kempe is not strong enough to travel today," Brandun answered. "He's been very ill."

The look of annoyance that flashed across Thearl's face was unmistakable. Brandun noted wryly that Thearl was not as skilled in hiding his true emotions as Lord Bardaric.

"We have to stay on a few more days," Brandun insisted. "Can we assume your hospitality will continue?"

Thearl glared as he struggled to maintain his composure. Finally he smiled politely. "And how could I refuse the nephews of King Eadric? Consider my house your own." He rose stiffly and moved toward the stairs that led up to his chambers.

"We plan to check on our horses," Brandun called after him. "The fresh air will be good for Kempe." Thearl continued up the stairs as if he hadn't heard.

In the stable, Brandun fondled Sparke's silky nose, then turned to Kempe. "You are strong enough to ride today, aren't you?"

"Yes," Kempe assured him. "The food and night's rest helped tremendously. And now that Thearl expects us to stay a few days, it would be best to escape as soon as possible."

"A wonderful plan with only two problems," Brandun muttered. "When and how?"

Kempe rubbed Sherwynd's massive neck in silence, thinking.

"My lords," spoke a voice behind them. Startled, Brandun turned to see a stocky man of average height, with brown, windblown hair and beard, and deep brown eyes. "I am Marshal," the man informed them, bowing slightly, "the keeper of Thearl's horses. I would be honored to check the condition of your horses, since you seem to have travelled a ways."

"I thank you, sir," Kempe responded coolly, "but I know something about horse care myself, and I am quite capable of..."

Marshal ignored Kempe and bent to examine Sherwynd's forelegs. "Bend down here a moment, my lords, please — both of you."

Brandun crouched next to Marshal, watching Kempe and wondering if he would put up with being ignored. But before Kempe could say more, Marshal began to speak in a low voice, moving his hands up and down the horse's forelegs and lifting each hoof to check underneath.

"Thearl is a tyrant! He loves power, and cruelly controls his villeins' lives. We are his tenants, and he claims the right to do what he wants with us. Larke is my daughter. She is stubborn and strong — a skilled rider. Thearl thinks her a fine challenge, and that's why he wants her for a wife. He wants to break her spirit, and control her."

Marshal's teeth were clenched as he turned to examine Sparke's hind legs. Brandun felt the same anger that had risen when Thearl yanked Larke away from him the day before. "Runaway tenants are severely punished if caught," Marshall continued. "I can't consider escaping with my family — I have six children! We would never make it. And Larke would have a hard time on her own. She is not experienced in traveling."

Marshal looked into Brandun's eyes. "Larke has dreams," he said. "Dreams that tell her things. She saw both of you in a dream before you arrived, and thinks you are the ones to help her escape." Brandun looked at Kempe, bewildered. With pleading eyes, Marshal also turned to Kempe.

Kempe blinked rapidly in confusion. "We are on an important quest for the kingdom," he explained. "To have to protect a girl would be — it would severely jeopardize our mission."

"We've got to help her," Brandun argued, his voice rising.

"Quiet!" Kempe hissed. "You can't just think with your heart, little cousin. The head must be involved, too."

Brandun frowned, clutching some straw and throwing it.

"I can help you escape," Marshal told them earnestly, leaning toward Kempe. "Perhaps she could go with you to another town, and someone would take her in."

Kempe sighed and was silent a moment. Brandun continued to throw bits of straw and scowl.

"You realize," Kempe pointed out, "that you could be severely punished for helping us."

Marshal grasped Kempe's shoulders. "He won't kill me. I'm too valuable a servant. And no torture he could inflict would be more agonizing than watching my daughter be used and controlled in that monster's house for the rest of her life."

Brandun held his breath, watching Kempe look into Marshal's eyes as the seconds dragged by. "All right," Kempe agreed quietly. "How can we leave without being followed?"

Brandun exhaled through grinning lips.

Back in their dark sleeping chamber, with a half moon casting faint shadows, Brandun fidgeted restlessly on his mattress. "Don't worry," Kempe whispered next to him. "Thearl thinks we plan to stay for days, and I've been acting very weak."

"I know," Brandun muttered. "But he's always watching us."

Both bolted up as the door quietly opened. The thin bald servant who had spoken to Brandun the night before

50

slipped into the room. "The t-t-time is g-g-good," he stuttered softly. "Th-thearl's asssssleep — y-your rrrroom's n-n-not g-guarded." He motioned for them to follow, and led them down a winding stairway to the kitchen. From the door to the great hall came the hushed breathing of most of the household staff as they lay asleep, wrapped in their cloaks. They tip-toed across the kitchen, grateful for the bit of moonlight through a window that kept them from clattering into pots or plates.

The servant opened a door and motioned Brandun and Kempe out. Marshal stood waiting for them, dressed in a cloak. Brandun turned and waved to the servant, who smiled before he closed the door. Stealthily, they followed Marshal to a barn behind the stable where hay was stored. Inside, crouched among the prickly piles, he spoke to them.

"There are two guards walking the grounds, but they're not on alert. Thearl really doesn't expect anything tonight. After dark, I said I had to attend to a limping horse, and spent some time in the stable. I switched your horses to the stalls furthest from the manor, and put some of Thearl's own where they used to be. Your horses are saddled and loosely tied. My brother is helping me. The two of us will mount the horses that stand in place of yours, and ride toward the road. I wish there were no moon tonight, but I think with our cloaks on, it won't be easy to tell we are not young princes. When the guards follow us, you must take your horses and ride quickly through the hayfield behind the manor to the woods. Larke is waiting at the edge of the woods now, on my own horse. Ride east along the edge of the woods, and keep going as long as you possibly can. Do you understand?"

Brandun and Kempe nodded.

"Good," said Marshal. He put a hand on each of their shoulders. "I'm forever grateful." Pulling his cloak tighter around him, he slipped out into the night. Brandun and Kempe followed him to the back of the stables, where Marshal's brother waited. They stood close against the stable wall while the two cloaked figures went in among the horses. Brandun's heart pounded, and he barely breathed. When he heard the hoofbeats of the horses heading toward the road, a chill crept up his spine. Soon the shouts of the guards sounded out of the darkness. Running footsteps grew louder, and the guards entered the stables to get horses for the chase. Brandun closed his eyes and prayed they wouldn't pick Sparke and Sherwynd. They chose horses closer to the manor.

As the guards clattered toward the road, shouting to arouse more help, Brandun and Kempe dashed in, loosed the ropes on their horses, and led them quickly out into the night and behind the stable. Both mounted without stopping the horses, and urged them back through the short-cropped hayfield toward the shadowy woods. It seemed miles that they rode, exposed under the moonlight. Brandun kept glancing back to see if they were being followed, but saw only the menacing silhouette of Thearl's manor.

As the woods drew closer, Brandun could make out a vague figure ahead, and when they were near enough,

the figure became a girl on a horse. Brandun and Kempe
swerved east at the edge of the woods. Larke kicked her
horse's flanks and followed.

ChapteR 7

The three riders made their way along the edge of the woods until dawn, then entered the cover of the forest and continued on more slowly. The tension they felt, wondering if they would be followed, left little energy for speaking, so the ride was a quiet one.

Brandun watched Kempe ahead of him, tall in his saddle, blazing the trail. When he glanced behind him, he saw Larke, serious and afraid, and wished he could think of something to say. They stopped at a trickle of a stream to let the horses drink and nibble at some foliage. Larke silently passed out food from her saddle bags.

"This stream must flow to the river," Kempe observed. "It would be best to travel closer to the river, so we'd always be sure of water. We're lucky this lovely lady thought to bring food."

Larke smiled faintly, her hazel eyes soft. Brandun struggled within himself for something to say — something that would make those eyes turn toward him — but all he could manage was, "Yes, thank you," and that only brought a glance.

They pressed onward all day, veering north in hopes of coming back to the river, but stayed in the forest. As dusk shadowed the sky, they picked a sheltered clearing where they wearily dismounted to spend the night. Kempe lowered himself to the ground against a tree, sighing with exhaustion. "Are you all right?" Brandun asked, and then quickly explained to Larke, "He's been ill."

"Oh — was this ride too much for you?" Larke asked, her voice full of concern.

"No," Kempe responded with a grin. "I'm just ready for a good rest and some more food. Is there any left?"

Larke dug into her bag and brought some bread to Kempe. Timidly she touched his forehead. "No fever," she said.

Kempe smiled. "I'm not sick — just not back to full strength yet."

Brandun watched, wishing sorely that *he* had been sick, or had a cut or bruise that Larke might tend. "Tomorrow, will we try to cross back over the road to the river?" he interrupted.

Kempe pulled a knife from his belt and began to whittle a thick stick. "Yes," he said. "If Thearl's men followed the road east, they'll be well ahead of us. I think we can risk a dash across the open fields."

Brandun noticed tears welling up in Larke's eyes. "What's the matter?" he asked.

Larke sat down and hugged her knees. "I'm afraid of what Thearl will do to my father when he catches him — I hope he'll leave my family alone." She sniffed and let her tears spill over. Then she wiped her face and laughed, a dimple appearing in each cheek. "Father wouldn't believe how quiet I've been all day. He's always trying to stop me from speaking my mind so much. But now, why don't we pass some time finding out about each other? Father told me you are King Eadric's nephews, and I've never been so close to princes before. Tell me about your lives and your quest."

Much to Brandun's annoyance, Kempe took charge of the telling of Eadric's death, and of their quest. "Many years ago," Kempe told her, "this kingdom had fallen into the hands of treacherous rulers, who used their subjects wickedly for their own gains. Daegmund, our ancestor and Thearl's, was a subject in this kingdom. He had lost all hope of a decent life here, so he attempted an escape with his family over the Jahaziel Mountains to the east. It was in the Jahaziel Mountains that he came upon the Temple of Wisdom, and was told that he was the one who could save his fellow subjects from wicked rulers. He had the ability to receive true wisdom, to overthrow the evil government, and to rule a new kingdom with honesty and honor.

"Daegmund spent many weeks in the Jahaziel Mountains, learning to be a wise ruler, and many more weeks traveling about the kingdom, secretly raising an army. The treacherous rulers had had the people under their thumbs for so long that they were not prepared for such a large uprising. The rebellion was successful, and the people joyously proclaimed Daegmund king, because he had led them, and because he carried the golden scepter that had been given to him at the Temple of Wisdom. They renamed the kingdom 'Haefen', which means 'a haven'.

"But Daegmund wanted to make sure Haefen never again fell under the power of evil men. He wanted only those with sufficient wisdom to inherit the throne. So he established that no one could be proclaimed heir to the throne until that person had first traveled to the Jahaziel Mountains to find the Temple of Wisdom, for only those who want to rule with true wisdom will be given a golden scepter at that Temple. The scepter is the sign. He who comes home carrying the golden scepter will be the next king."

"But you are both searching for the Temple," Larke cut in. "I suppose you both would want to rule with true wisdom. Is it the one who gets there first who receives the scepter?"

Brandun and Kempe looked at each other. "We don't know," Brandun admitted. "The custom has been that the eldest prince goes first, alone, and the next goes only if the first can't find the Temple. Eadric wanted us to go together, because he wanted an heir established as soon as possible, but we don't know how it will work if we find the Temple. I think Eadric was going to tell us, but he died before —"

Brandun choked on his words and looked at the ground. Quickly, Larke reached over and grasped his hand. Her fingers felt cool against his palm. The three were silent for a few moments, and then Larke struck up more conversation. She listened, her eyes shining with admiration, as Kempe charmingly answered her questions about himself and life at the king's castle. At sixteen, Kempe could have been married — most noblemen

57

were, having had their marriages arranged years before. But Eadric and Aeldra wished to allow Kempe and Brandun some choice in the matter, and Kempe hadn't shown serious interest in any one girl. He simply charmed *every* girl that he met, and it seemed to Brandun that his older cousin could have any girl he chose. Brandun hoped that he wouldn't choose Larke.

When Kempe handed Larke the beautifully carved fish he had fashioned from the thick stick, she gasped with delight. Brandun moodily scratched the forest floor with another stick, until Larke finally turned to him. "And what about you, Brandun. How old are you?"

Brandun instinctively tried to smooth down his brown curls. Thirteen sounded unbearably young, especially since he now knew that Larke was fourteen. "I'll be fourteen in the fall," he answered truthfully. Then, wanting to change the subject and not talk about himself in Kempe's shadow, he asked her, "What's your life like? And what's all this about a dream?"

Resting her chin on her knees, Larke smiled. "I have two loving parents who became Thearl's tenants in order to have a place to raise their family. They didn't realize until too late what kind of a man he is. I have two older sisters, both married and one a mother, who are much prettier and more feminine than I am."

You're pretty, Brandun wanted to say, but didn't.

"My mother tries to teach me weaving and needlework, but I'm so clumsy at it. I love horses and riding, and working outdoors with my father. I have three younger brothers, who make enough noise for all of us.

As for my dreams..." She stopped and furrowed her brow, as if trying to decide what to say. "My mother comes from a long line of women who are interested in dreams. Mother likes to help people find meaning in their dreams.

"Sometimes I have dreams that are different from the ordinary kind. They are very vivid and real — full of sensation. Whenever I've had one of those, it's come true not long after."

"Come true?" Brandun asked.

Larke lifted her head. "The thing that had happened in the dream happens in real life."

Brandun and Kempe were silent a moment. "That's never happened to me," Brandun remarked.

"No," said Kempe, shaking his head. "I've never heard of such a thing."

"I know," Larke sighed. "I'd like it better if people believed me, but it doesn't matter. Mother and Father believe me. Mother calls it a gift. In any case, ever since Thearl announced that I would be his wife when I turned fifteen, I've been desperate for a way to escape. Then, about a week ago, I had one of those vivid dreams. I dreamed of two young men riding up to Thearl's manor, one on a gray horse, and one on a bay. I could smell the horses, and hear the jingle of their harness. I could see every wrinkle in the fine blue clothing of the older rider, and the glow of sunlight on his auburn hair. Every brown curl on the younger rider's head was clear, and the question in his blue-green eyes as he looked right at me. The two dream riders were you, and a few days later, you arrived. I knew you were the ones to help me."

Brandun's skin tingled as he listened to the description, and remembered looking into Larke's eyes when he first saw her. He glanced at Kempe through the deepening darkness, who shrugged his shoulders, puzzled.

"Well," said Larke, "let's get some sleep. I've never slept on the ground, but I'm so tired I might not even notice."

Kempe stood up and opened his saddle bag. Pulling out a red woolen cloak, he gallantly presented it to Larke. "Our steward packed me two cloaks, but I only need one tonight. Perhaps it will make the ground a little softer for you."

"Oh, thank you," breathed Larke, looking up at him with a grateful smile. Brandun gripped his forehead in frustration, wondering why he hadn't thought to offer *his* extra cloak. Pulling his own around him tightly, he lay down and stared up into the black tree branches, listening to the continuous shrill music of the crickets.

In what seemed like an instant later, Brandun was startled out of sound sleep by a scream. He and Kempe scrambled, bleary-eyed, into a sitting position, and saw that the scream had come from Larke. Breathing in frightened gulps, she sat stiff with terror, staring out into the forest. "Larke!" Brandun exclaimed as he and Kempe crawled over to her. "What is it?"

"Did you see someone?" Kempe asked, peering into the black forest, his hand moving to his sword hilt.

Larke struggled to slow her breathing and calm herself. Finally she managed to tell them, "It was a dream."

"Oh — you had a bad dream," Brandun sympathized.

"Not just a dream," she insisted shakily. "One of those special dreams I was telling you about. It was — dreadfully real. I was in a room that was damp and gray, with a bed, and a chest, and wood shavings on the floor. I could smell the wetness and the wood. Then a powerful arm gripped me around the waist, and Thearl was laughing right in my ear, his beard scraping my neck." She covered her mouth with her hands, whimpering with fear.

Kempe put an arm around her shoulders. "It was a dream," he said gently. "You're safe in the forest with us."

Brandun touched her arm. "We'll protect you, Larke," he assured her. "We won't let Thearl get you."

Trembling, Larke lowered herself back down onto Kempe's red cloak. "I've never had a dream that vivid that didn't come true," she muttered.

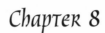

Chapter 8

The next morning the sky was gray and overcast, and the clouds darkened and thickened as the day wore on. The three riders picked their way through the forest, veering north toward the main road. None of them were eager to ride across the open road and fields, but Larke's small supply of ale was gone, and they had to get back near the river.

By afternoon they reached the edge of the forest, and could see the road. They stopped and scanned the area for any signs of horsemen. The increasing wind billowed their cloaks behind them, and tossed the horses' manes and tails. Brandun looked questioningly at Kempe.

"At the moment, there's no one in sight," said Kempe. "I think we ought to go across one at a time. Three riders together would catch the eyes of Thearl's men more quickly. I'll go first, and when I disappear down the slope toward the river, it's time for the next one of you. If I see anyone, I'll raise my sword, and you two go back and hide in the forest."

Kempe touched Sherwynd's flanks with his heels, and the horse stepped forward. Brandun and Larke watched the figure of Kempe grow smaller as he crossed the wide field and then the road, finally to vanish over the slope.

"You ought to go next," Brandun told Larke. "It wouldn't be good for you to be alone if Thearl's men appeared. Follow Kempe's path, and raise your arm in the air if you see anyone on the road."

Larke nodded and started across the field, her long braid whipping behind her. When she, too, had disappeared over the slope without raising her arm, Brandun gave Sparke a gentle kick. "Let's go, boy," he urged, and the horse cantered forward. Once in the open, Brandun felt as exposed as he had on that moonlit night, escaping from Thearl's manor. Open fields stretched to the east and the west as far as he could see, and the downslope to the river seemed an unbearable distance away. He felt he must be visible for miles, and turned his head from side to side, frantically watching for signs of movement on the road or in the fields. Finally, he galloped across the worn dirt road and soon after descended a grassy hill until he saw the churning river, with Kempe and Larke waiting anxiously beside it. They smiled when they saw him.

"Success!" Brandun called triumphantly as he halted Sparke beside them. Then he glanced up at the blackening sky and remarked, "I suppose it's not a good day for travelers to be on the road."

Larke had dismounted to fill a wooden bowl with water, and she handed it to Brandun.

"I think Thearl and his men would be well beyond this point by now," said Kempe confidently. "Now we must be careful not to run into them if they turn back."

There was no forest to hide in here, but the small valley they were in kept the riders out of sight of the road. After Larke had mounted again, they traveled east along the river while the wind beat at their backs. Thunder rumbled behind them. "I think the storm's going to be bad," Brandun yelled to Kempe. "We'll need shelter!"

Kempe nodded, and all three riders urged their mounts into a canter. After a few minutes, Kempe turned his head back and shouted, "I see a town ahead!"

Over a slope on the other side of the river, a town wall appeared. They rode on until they saw a dirt road leading away from the main road. It led to a wooden bridge. Clattering over the bridge while thunder ripped the sky, they headed for the open town gate. Large raindrops pelted their uncovered heads, and turned into a torrential downpour as they entered the town. Kempe pointed to a building that displayed a pole and banner in front of it — the sign of an inn offering freshly brewed ale. The riders quickly dismounted and led their horses into the adjoining stable.

The warm smell of horses and dry hay greeted Brandun's nose as they stepped under the sheltering roof. He led Sparke to a stall, shivering in his wet clothing as he brought armfuls of hay to the hungry animal. He untied his saddlebags and tossed them across his shoulder. "All right, let's go in," said Kempe when he and Larke had also attended to their horses.

"Wait," said Larke, grabbing his arm.

"What is it?" Kempe asked, puzzled.

She was shivering with more than just cold, and

spoke quickly. "What if the room in my dream is in this inn — the room where Thearl will catch me?"

Kempe's puzzled expression changed to one of impatience. "Larke, a dream does not make something come about. Brandun and I are here to protect you, and Thearl will have gone on toward the Jahaziel Mountains to find us."

Larke scowled and turned away from his unbelieving words, crossing her arms. "It was not *just* a dream," she insisted.

Brandun felt unsure. It seemed strange to make decisions based on a dream, and yet Larke's earnestness made him hesitate. "Her dream about us came true," he pointed out. "Maybe we should think about it."

Kempe flashed him an annoyed look. "We need to spend tonight out of the rain. I know we must always be on the look out, but let's base our decisions on reality, shall we?" He turned abruptly and headed through the rain to the inn entrance.

Gritting his teeth in frustration, Brandun looked down and kicked some hay. Kempe had made his decision. Brandun looked up at Larke's frightened face, and gently took her by the elbow. "Come on," he coaxed. "We'll keep our eyes sharp, and stay right near you."

The stormy wind gusted through the door as they entered the inn. The large, dimly lit room smelled of smoky warm cooking, and damp clothes and bodies. Large boards set on trestles formed long tables, around which boisterous men and a few women enjoyed food and ale and lively conversation. Kempe approached them from the far end of the room. "The innkeeper has a room for us tonight," he informed them, "and I've paid for that and a meal. Let's sit down." They found an empty space on a bench, and sat waiting at the table for their food. Carefully, Brandun studied the faces of each person in the room, but no one seemed to be looking at them.

A man sitting next to Brandun talked loudly over his meat and ale. "This town life, now there's something!" he said. "People in a free town like this can live as they please, and come and go as they want to. Me, I'm only allowed out of my village because I'm on an errand for my lord. And he'll grace my back with some lashes if I don't complete my mission in an efficient and timely fashion! Sometimes it seems no better than prison."

A man across from him shook his head. "I'm sorry for you, friend. I'm fortunate enough to have a lord who never beats us, and is mostly decent and fair. But I, too, am a tenant, indebted to stay in my village and pay rent to my lord with money, goods, and service as long as I live. My life is not terrible, but I often wonder what it would be like to live as a free man, and choose my own life and livelihood."

Brandun listened with interest as the two men described their lives to each other, finished their meal, and then rose and left the hall. Now alone at the table with his friends, Brandun leaned over to speak softly to Larke and Kempe. "Can it really be right," he asked them, "that a lord own the lives of his villeins? I've never thought about it before."

Kempe let out his breath in exasperation. "Why waste thought on such things, Brandun? It's always been the way."

"But Larke was not even allowed to resist a miserable marriage, and her father was not allowed to protect her," Brandun argued.

"It is never right for a lord to be cruel to his tenants," Kempe reasoned, pointing a finger at Brandun. "If he is, he must be stopped, and answer to the king."

"But even if a lord is *not* cruel to his villeins," Brandun persisted, "is it really right that he make all the big decisions in their lives for them? Don't you and I value our right to live as we want to?"

"Do you really choose?" Larke interjected suddenly. "Are you not born to royalty, and expected to remain in positions of honor?" Brandun and Kempe stared at her in surprise, and Brandun remembered his wish to be a simple peasant when he and Ladroc had talked about Lord Bardaric's scheme. But before either one could answer, the innkeeper waddled over with trays of meat and bread. He was a large man, with a fringe of graying black hair around his bald head, and a long, greasy mustache. His face was covered with perspiration from the heat of the kitchen.

"Here you are," he said amiably, "and your ale's coming soon. You're awfully young to be traveling from town to town. Have you come far?"

"Yes, quite far," Kempe answered smoothly, and then changed the subject. "We are tired, and would like to be shown to our room as soon as we've eaten. Is that possible?"

"Oh, yes, of course," the innkeeper agreed. "As I told you, I've only got one empty room, but it's got two mattresses, so the young lady can have her own." He winked at Larke, and she blushed.

After the three young travellers had filled their stomachs, they followed the innkeeper up a narrow staircase to the sleeping rooms. Brandun and Kempe let Larke use the room first to change into dry clothes from her saddle bag, and then she let them do the same. They hung their wet clothes on pegs on the walls. "Well, here I am, dressed as a prince again," Brandun commented, looking down at his dark green traveling outfit, and then at the clothes from Lufu, hanging on the wall. "Perhaps we'd be less noticeable if we were dressed like commoners."

Kempe shook his head. "We didn't think of that when we left the castle, and neither did Ladroc — there wasn't time. Let's get some sleep, and try to leave early." Brandun blew out the candle the innkeeper had left on the floor, and lay down beside Kempe on one of the straw-filled mattresses. In the dark he could just make out the shape of Larke lying on the other mattress. Brandun listened awhile to the shuffling of people in the hallway, making their way to their rooms, and then the inn was quiet except for Kempe's deep, steady breathing. Kempe never had trouble falling asleep — it took him only minutes. Brandun often lay awake for an hour or more, as thoughts and wonderings buzzed through his mind like flying insects. Just as he felt his mind beginning to relax, a soft whisper startled him.

"Brandun." He turned and sensed, rather than saw,

Larke crouching beside his mattress. "I just wanted to tell you," she whispered, "that while you were changing, I peeked into all the rooms in the inn — the other guests were still down in the eating hall — and none were the room in my dream. I think I'm safe here, and — thank you for believing me. I wish Kempe would."

"He's just — very practical," Brandun explained, warm with pleasure that she appreciated something in him that Kempe didn't have.

"I know," she sighed. "And I guess it's good that he is. Well, good night."

"Good night." Brandun listened to her bare footsteps, and to the crunching of the straw mattress as she lay down. Then he drifted into a deep quiet sleep, hearing nothing until Larke's voice, urgent and desperate, suddenly pierced the dark stillness.

"No. No! I can't! NO!"

Chapter 9

Brandun and Kempe bolted up in shocked confusion, just as they had in the forest. In the pitch blackness of the cloudy night, Brandun couldn't see for certain if Larke was on her mattress. Beside him, Kempe called out hoarsely, "Larke?" and was answered by shuddering sobs. Brandun crawled toward her, stretching his hand out to feel his way. Soon his hand hit the edge of her mattress, and then was on her trembling shoulder. Larke was sitting up, clutching her knees to her chest.

"Ohh," she moaned between sobs. "Another dream, so awful and real! There was a man. He had his back turned toward me. He terrified me, even though he never looked at me. He was going to do something horrible, and I knew I was the only one who could stop him. I felt so small, and afraid. He was so big..." She put her face in her hands and cried some more.

A faint light glowed outside their room, and then a heavy fist pounded on the door. "What goes on in there?" demanded a bellowing voice. The door swung open to reveal the large silhouette of the innkeeper holding a lighted candle. Brandun could here the murmuring of others in the hallway.

70

Kempe leaped up and approached the innkeeper. "The young lady had a nightmare," he explained, "but we are taking care of her. I'm sorry if this has disturbed you and your other guests."

The innkeeper cast his candlelight on Larke. "Is this true?" he asked her.

"Yes," she managed to answer weakly. "I had a frightening dream."

"All right, then," said the innkeeper. Turning back into the hallway, he called out, "Nothing to worry about — just a girl having a bad dream." The yellow glow faded as he walked away, and after more murmuring and shuffling from people in other rooms, all was quiet and dark again. Brandun and Kempe sat on the edge of Larke's mattress.

"Well," said Kempe after a few moments' silence, "I think it's best if we get some sleep now." He waited another awkward moment for some kind of answer, and when none came, he rose and made his way back to his bed.

Brandun waited in the stillness, then spoke softly. "Larke?"

She grabbed his arm. "Awful things are going to happen to me," she said, her voice trembling.

Brandun felt her nails digging into his arm. "Can we stop them from happening?"

"I don't know," she whispered, releasing her grip. "I've never had this kind of dream be so frightening. I'm so — tired."

"Lie down," Brandun coaxed. "Kempe and I will

stay with you every minute." After Larke shakily lowered herself onto the mattress, Brandun started to rise,
but she grabbed his sleeve. Brandun sat quietly on the
edge of her mattress until her breathing told him she
was finally asleep. Then he crawled back to his place
beside Kempe.

When morning light and the song of birds roused
Brandun, Larke, and Kempe, they washed hands and
faces in the provided bowl of water, gathered their
belongings, and descended the narrow stairway to the
dining hall. "I'm glad this building wasn't the one in my
dream," Larke said as they sat at a long trestle table. "I'll
feel safer if we stay out of buildings for the rest of our
journey." She glanced at Kempe and blushed. "I know
you think I'm silly..." she began.

Kempe shrugged. "I know you have a lot to be afraid
of. I think perhaps the dreams are your fears playing
themselves in your head."

Larke shook her head slightly in frustration as the
innkeeper approached their table with bread and ale. He
greeted them, placed the food and drink before them, and
sat down on their bench. "I hope you won't hurry off,"
he said in a friendly manner. "I don't often get such
young guests staying at my inn. It's refreshing! Would
you perhaps join me in my living quarters for some wine,
and tell me about your travels?"

"Thank you, but no," Kempe declined cordially.
"We have to be on our way."

The innkeeper looked disappointed, and drummed
his fingers on the tabletop. Then, as his guests ate, he

pulled a small knife from his belt, and a piece of wood from a pouch that hung from the belt. Thoughtfully, he whittled at the wood, which was already partially smoothed and formed into a bird.

Kempe looked over with interest. "That's quite good," he commented. "Do you carve often?"

The innkeeper grinned at him from under the greasy mustache. "Whenever I find a moment," he said. "It helps me relax." He paused, and then asked, "Would you like to see the rest of my work? I have quite a few pieces in my room."

Kempe chewed his last bite of bread and took a large swallow of ale. "I'd like to have a quick look," he told Brandun and Larke, "to get some fresh ideas for my own carving."

Brandun could think of no reason to object, none that Kempe would see as sensible. "I suppose it's all right," he said. "Is it, Larke?"

Larke shrugged. "A quick look," she agreed, though he could sense she wanted to leave. They all rose with the innkeeper, and he led them toward the far end of the dining hall, away from the kitchen and the stairway that led upstairs.

"Your room is not upstairs?" Brandun asked, surprised. Most businessmen lived in quarters above their places of business.

"I wanted all those rooms for my guests," the innkeeper explained, ushering Kempe and then Larke hurriedly through an open doorway at the end of the room. "So I built this one for myself. It's a bit damp right now — some rain leaked in the windows during the storm." He placed a hand firmly on Brandun's back and pushed him through the doorway.

Larke had checked every room upstairs, but they hadn't noticed this one. Within a moment Brandun took in the sight of a gray room with a bed, a chest, shavings on the floor, and the smell of dampness and wood. He turned in horror to Larke, whose face had gone white. She barely had a second to choke out, "My dream!" The open door behind them slammed shut and a tall figure pounced on Larke from behind, grabbing her waist with a powerful arm and laughing in gleeful triumph. From behind Lord Thearl leaped one of his attendants, armed with a large sword. He planted himself with his back toward Larke and Thearl, his sword held ready to strike if Brandun or Kempe approached. The two princes reached for their own swords.

"Wait!" yelled Thearl, quickly drawing his own dagger and holding it at Larke's throat. Brandun and Kempe froze, and Thearl laughed again, his black beard against Larke's cheek and neck. "I'd rather have my bride alive," he shouted wryly, "but if I must nick her a bit to keep her, so be it. It might teach her a lesson — her father certainly learned his!" Larke, who had kept silent and still, closed her eyes in anguish and moaned softly. "Innkeeper!" Thearl ordered. "Fetch the rest of my men!"

Watching the innkeeper make his way to the door, Brandun's fury heated to boiling. "Worm!" he shouted in disgust. "You set this trap!"

The innkeeper turned and glared at him. "Your majesty," he said coolly. "I was doing my duty to help return a runaway villein. I've done nothing against the law."

"And no doubt you were paid well for your fine performance of duty," Brandun snarled as the innkeeper left the room. Thearl laughed again.

"Yes, money makes people very cooperative," he said, backing out of the room and dragging Larke with him. "And now that I have recovered my property, your majesties are free to go. I will not this time demand retribution for being wronged by the royal family, but I hope in the future, you will respect my rights." Three more men with drawn swords appeared at the doorway. "Hold them here until I am gone," Thearl barked at them. "You know where to meet me. And as for you," he said, glaring at Brandun and Kempe, "if you pursue us, it will be the worse for Larke."

The two princes silently faced the four drawn swords. Thearl galloped by the window with Larke in front of him on his ebony black horse, leading Larke's golden brown one by its reins. Brandun trembled with rage as the minutes dragged by like hours, and the murmuring of the crowd in the dining hall rose and fell. Finally, one of the men gave a sharp order to the rest, and they all backed out of the room. Within minutes they were outside and on horseback, clattering out of town toward the main road.

As the sound of hoofbeats faded in the distance, Brandun's trembling rage only grew, and his clenched fists grew tighter. He turned to unleash it at the only other person in the room. "You didn't believe her!" he screamed at Kempe. "You didn't believe her dream, and you let that scum of an innkeeper lead us right into Thearl's trap! All our efforts, and her father's punishment — it was all for nothing! And now Larke has to suffer as that monster's wife for the rest of her life!" He flung himself at Kempe and shoved with all his might, sending him sprawling backward until he hit hard against the wall. Startled and then angry, Kempe regained his balance and strode forward. He gave Brandun a quick, forceful push on the chest, and the younger prince fell with a thud onto the hardened dirt floor.

"Don't be a fool, Brandun," he shouted. "If you want to help Larke, stop acting like a maniac and think about what we can do next!" Brandun turned his face to the ground and pounded it with his fist until his hand throbbed. Then he lay still awhile, breathing deeply to calm himself.

When finally he lifted his head, Brandun saw that Kempe was sitting on the floor against the wall with his face in his hands. He sat up and called out softly, "Kempe." Kempe removed his hands to reveal a face full of weary confusion.

"I didn't believe her," he said, staring at the wall opposite him. "I thought her fears were running away with her." Kempe was quiet for a few minutes, then rose and said, "We'll follow them."

Brandun stood up, too. "Kempe, I'm sorry," he said. "I was just so upset, I exploded. I know you care about Larke."

Kempe looked at him. "Yes, I do," he said. "Let's leave this place. We'll think what to do as we travel."

They rode west, back toward Thearl's manor, at a slow pace, not wanting to come upon Thearl and his men in the daylight. The sun beat down warmly, drying the moisture from the heavy storm. As evening approached, they urged their horses into a quick trot, keeping their eyes out for the glow of a campfire. The forest had been thick to the south of the road throughout the day's journey, but now a woods was forming also to the north, along the river. The sun set ahead of them, surrounded by soft orange and pink, and the moon appeared, brilliant white in a clear, dark sky. They continued on as the glow of the sunset completely disappeared, and the stars began to show themselves. Brandun looked to the north and Kempe to the south, scanning the darkness until their eyes ached.

After a half hour's travel in the dark, Brandun spotted a flicker of light ahead in the woods toward the river. Quickly, he signaled Kempe, and they slowed their mounts to a walk. Drawing nearer, they dismounted and left the horses to graze near the road while they entered the woods and stealthily approached the firelight on foot. The rush of the river, along with voices and laughter from around the campfire, grew louder, and Brandun was grateful for the noise that would help drown out the soft rustle of their approach. He and Kempe silently drew their swords and pressed themselves behind two trees. From there they could make out through the foliage a crackling fire, the shadowy figures of Thearl and his men, and the pale form of Larke, sitting against a tree with her wrists tied behind it.

Chapter 10

Brandun's breath caught in his throat at the sight of Larke. She looked small and helpless among Thearl's rough crew, and kept her face toward the ground.

"Let's get her out of there!" Brandun whispered urgently to Kempe.

"Yes, but wait," Kempe whispered back. "There are five armed men, all bigger than us. We have to plan carefully."

The two were silent a moment, thinking, and Brandun kept his eyes fixed on Larke. "If we wait into the night, probably only one will stay awake to guard her," Kempe murmured, half to himself. "If we could find a way to distract the guard without waking the others..."

Brandun continued to watch intently as Thearl's men shuffled around the fire, laughing and talking loudly and passing around pouches of wine. He felt panicky whenever Larke was hidden from his view for a moment. He determined which shadowy figure was Lord Thearl, and kept track of him. Soon Thearl made his way over to Larke. The dark-haired lord spoke some words to her, and he and his men burst into raucous laughter. Brandun felt his anger heating up, and grasped the hilt of his sword. Kempe's murmuring words drifted past him — he heard only the ugly laughter. Then Thearl crouched beside Larke and, taking her long braid in his hand, yanked it roughly downward to force her to look up at him. As the faintest trace of Larke's cry of pain pierced through the callous voices and reached Brandun's ears, his anger boiled over, and he plunged into action.

"Brandun, no!" Kempe cried out, but Brandun was already crashing through the shrubs and branches, sword drawn and face red with fury. He saw Thearl and his men jerk around, squinting to try and make out what was approaching them from the dark forest. In his burning mind, Brandun saw how the rescue would go — how he would knock aside the startled men just enough to lunge toward Larke and cut her ropes. She could escape while he turned to keep Thearl and his men busy by stabbing at them and dodging their blows, just as he had learned in battle skills training. Then of course Kempe would follow, surprising them again from behind....

Brandun hurtled himself into the clearing with a ferocious yell and lunged at Lord Thearl, but in a flash from the right, one of Thearl's men advanced and swung a heavy arm against his stomach, knocking the breath out of him and doubling him over. An instant later, a thudding blow to the back of his head made sparks explode before his eyes, and Brandun collapsed onto the forest floor in a daze. He faintly heard Thearl bellow out, "Go find the other one!" Then all went black and quiet.

When Brandun woke up, the throbbing ache in his head made the firelight seem to pulsate in front of him, and the noise from Thearl and his men throbbed with the pain. He groaned and tried to move, but found that his wrists were tied behind his back, and that tight ropes chafed his ankles as well. Prickly twigs and shoots dug into his back. He rolled onto his side and huddled there miserably. Not far from him, Kempe lay on his back, tied up as well, and beyond Kempe sat Larke, still secured to the same tree. Brandun painfully turned his head toward the sound of a horse's whicker, and saw that Sparke and Sherwynd were tethered near the river with Thearl's own horses.

"More wine before we retire," Thearl announced loudly, holding up two more full skins. "We have much to celebrate tonight; the recovery of my dear wife-to-be," he said with a wry smile, "and the easy capture of the princes who tried to take her from me. Since they did not choose to leave us alone, now they will serve me." Thearl laughed scornfully. "You fools," he scoffed at Brandun and Kempe. "We knew you would follow us. Larke, here, makes lovely bait, and I'm so glad you noticed our campfire. We built it in this secluded place so we could seize you without witnesses. Now you will take me to the Temple of Wisdom and to the golden scepter, which will be mine as soon as you two meet with some convenient accident. No one can contest my right to the throne if I have that scepter. It was Daegmund himself who decreed it would be the sign!" Thearl handed the wineskins to his men and fetched two more. "None for you, Fitch," he said, pointing to one of his men. "I want you to keep your wits about you and guard our prisoners." Fitch scowled and bit off a hunk of bread from the loaf in his hand. Brandun's empty stomach growled at the sight of it.

"A toast," Thearl cried out, when his other three men had their wine, "to the next king of Haefen!" His men cheered, and they all gulped wine heartily, fetching more full skins when those were empty.

"Kempe," Brandun called weakly. "They caught you!"

Kempe clenched his teeth and snarled. "Of course they did, idiot! Do you think I'd have any chance against five armed men? I was so *shocked* by your rush into their midst that I didn't turn to run quickly enough, and they caught me before I could reach my horse. What insanity took over you? Did you actually think we'd have a chance, rushing in without a plan? Thanks to your foolish charge, we're lying tied up, when we could have been hiding out, waiting for a chance to free Larke."

The pain in Brandun's head and stomach increased with Kempe's words. *He's right,* he thought in agony. *I caused this whole disaster.* He closed his eyes, and the weight of his guilt made it hard to breath. Suddenly something hard hit his nose, and his eyes sprung open. A chunk of bread lay a foot from his face, and Fitch stood over him. "Thearl says to feed you," he growled, "or else you won't be much good for us tomorrow." Hunger momentarily pushed all else out of Brandun's mind, and he struggled desperately to move his bound body over to the bread. He drew his knees up to press the food to his face and greedily tore pieces off with his teeth. Kempe was also engaged in trying to get bread into his mouth without hands, and Larke, in her sitting position, was gripping a loaf between her knees and leaning forward to take bites. Meanwhile, the laughter from Thearl and his men grew more drunken, and their movements more tipsy and staggering.

Brandun licked the last crumbs from the ground, and rolled wearily onto his back. He was startled into raising his head again when he heard Larke's high voice call out.

"Lord Thearl!"

Brandun rolled onto his side to watch Larke. She leaned forward and called Thearl's name two more times before he heard her. "Oh!" Thearl shouted with drunken joviality. "My dear lady calls! Perhaps the poor thing is lonely over there without me." His men burst into rowdy laughter as he struggled to his feet and staggered toward her, tripping once on a fallen branch. "And what does my lovely bride-to-be want?" he asked with mock gallantry.

Larke looked him in the face. "Thearl," she said calmly. "Please untie me."

Thearl laughed and nearly fell backwards. "I would like to," he told her. "But a vixen like you would try to run away, and that would be so annoying."

"I won't, Thearl," Larke continued intently. "I see it's useless to try and resist you. You're too — clever and powerful. I didn't feel ready to get married, but I realize it's time to grow up. You have the right to choose your wife, and I must obey. It's time for me to learn to — respect and love my husband."

Thearl lifted his eyebrows in surprise, then spread

his mouth into a drunken grin. "Well," he said, "have I humbled the cocky vixen at last?" He knelt in front of her. "Yes," he mused. "Perhaps I could let you loose awhile. Your would-be rescuers are tied up, and you have nowhere to run that we couldn't easily overtake you on horseback." He took her chin in one hand. "You could bring me some food, and rub my aching feet a while. That would be pleasant." Brandun felt nauseous, but squelched his anger.

"Yes," Larke replied, still meeting Thearl's gaze. "It's hopeless to escape, and it would be good for me to exercise — a change of heart." Thearl chuckled, and Larke smiled. "But I feel dreadful in these dirty, boyish clothes. If you would let me change, I have one dress in my saddle bag. It would help me feel more like a woman."

"Thearl," Fitch broke in, "don't untie her. She's trying to trick you."

Thearl rose unsteadily to his feet and glared at Fitch. "Who's in charge here?" he shouted angrily. "Are you telling *me* what to do with *my* villein and *my* chosen bride?" He swung a fist at Fitch but missed, and fell sprawling onto the ground. "The girl has no chance of escape," he sputtered, pushing himself up. "And besides," he added, grinning over at Larke, "it would please me to see her *dressed* as a woman for once." Thearl crawled back over to Larke, drew a dagger from his belt, and cut her ropes. Larke quickly unwrapped the ropes from her wrists and rubbed her chafed skin.

Brandun watched anxiously as she walked to her

horse tied by the river bank and rummaged through her saddle bag. What was she doing? He didn't think she would have brought a dress on this journey. Would she? Was she tricking Thearl so he would go easy on his prisoners until they could find a way to escape? Or had she finally given in to Thearl, thinking it hopeless to resist any more? Brandun's chest ached at the thought.

Larke pulled a small bundle of clothing from the saddle bag. "Now I must go and change," she stated, "alone, if you please."

"I beg your pardon, my lord," Fitch interrupted again, stepping forward. "Let me follow her to make sure she doesn't run away."

"You!" Thearl barked, pointing at Fitch in exasperation. "*You* will stay away from my woman! If anyone goes with her, it will be *me*!" Amidst shouts of agreement from his other three drunken companions, Thearl swaggered after Larke into the darkness of the forest.

Fitch scowled, helplessly watching them go. "Drunken fool," he muttered.

Brandun stared into the black night, listening to the crunch of Larke's and Thearl's footsteps. After a few tense minutes, an abrupt crash of breaking branches sounded out of the darkness, followed by a heavy thud and Thearl's irritated grunts and groans. Brandun saw Fitch hesitate, looking back and forth between the place the sound came from and his tied up prisoners, wondering whether to stay and guard Brandun and Kempe, or rush and see what had happened. Quickly Brandun began to struggle with his ropes, as if trying to escape. If

Larke had a plan, he wanted to give her time. Kempe saw him struggling and did the same.

Thearl's other three men floundered around in bewilderment, asking Fitch what had happened and what they should do. Cursing with frustration, Fitch gave Brandun and then Kempe swift, painful kicks in the stomach, warning them to be still. Finally, he ordered the other men to surround the prisoners, and keep watch. Brandun froze, hoping desperately that his three snarling, unsteady guards wouldn't tip over and drive their swords into him or Kempe.

Fitch ran into the forest, calling out Thearl's name. Thearl cursed loudly and told Fitch to hurry. "I've tripped over an idiotic branch," the drunken lord complained. "Come untangle my feet!" Brandun listened to the griping and commotion as Fitch helped Thearl to his feet, and then heard Thearl bellow out, "Larke!"

There was no answer.

Chapter 11

"Larke!" Thearl shouted again. Now back at the camp, his temper was rising. *"Come here now!"*

When there was still no answer, Thearl exploded. He screamed at Fitch to go and find her, and Brandun held his breath, fearing for her life. Fitch slashed his way unsuccessfully through the woods for a good half hour, only to return and tell Thearl it was hopeless to look for her in the dark — she had gotten too big a head start. Thearl gripped his forehead, growling through clenched teeth.

"She won't get far without a horse," Fitch reasoned. "We'll do a thorough search in the morning."

"In the morning," Thearl repeated, holding his head and sinking wearily to the ground. "I must sleep off this wine. Fitch, you stay awake and guard the prisoners. The rest of us are not fit." He crawled toward his cloak that lay spread at the other side of the camp fire. "When I catch that girl," he threatened, "I'll teach her *never* to disobey me again!"

Thearl's other three men crawled off to their own cloaks. Fitch watched them, and then spat in disgust. "Only one with enough wits to keep some kind of order," he muttered, "and I'm rewarded with the privilege of staying up all night." He kicked a nearby tree trunk and then sat down next to it, staring bitterly into the fire.

Brandun lay limp on the ground, but inwardly he writhed with emotion. The news that Larke had escaped filled him with excitement and terror. He turned his head and whispered weakly to Kempe, "Do you think she has a chance?"

Kempe shook his head gloomily. "I don't see how," he answered. "She's on foot, and Thearl is determined to catch her. He had little trouble finding us at the inn."

Kempe's tone of voice told Brandun he was still angry about his blundering rescue attempt. Guilt began to press heavily on him again. If he had waited for Kempe to think of a sensible plan, perhaps they really could have rescued Larke. Now she was alone in the darkness, running for her life. If caught, she would be severely punished, probably beaten. If by some chance she wasn't caught, she could run into other dangers and — Brandun realized he might never see her again. That thought burst into an ache of loneliness on top of his guilt, his fear, and all the pain in his weary body. He felt he was being swallowed up by despair, and suddenly, like a dam breaking, his grief for Eadric came flooding back — Eadric, who had been his protector, his guardian, his loving father. Eadric had always made everything all right and safe. What would Eadric think of him now? Eadric was the one who had gently warned him not to act compulsively, but to think things through. *I've failed, Eadric, and I've caused so much harm. I need you!*

Tears of pain and utter despair poured from Brandun's eyes. He fought to keep his sobs to a quiet whimper, and soon cried himself into an exhausted sleep.

In the silence of sleep, Brandun dreamed. He was on a soft mattress, under a feather quilt, feeling warm and blissfully comfortable. Muffled voices, as if from other rooms, drifted to his ears, and he propped himself up on an elbow to look around. The bed was Eadric's, with its colorful linen draperies. Brandun gazed around the room at the familiar wall tapestries, and the sunlight glowing through the stained glass picture of the Jahaziel Mountains. He sat up and looked toward the carved wooden door, wondering if he should go out and try to find someone.

Suddenly, the door swung open, and King Eadric strode into the room, looking strong and vibrant and richly dressed. Brandun's lower jaw dropped in dumbfounded amazement. Their eyes met, and Brandun's whole body tingled with excitement and longing. Eadric smiled and walked toward him, holding Brandun's gaze with every step. When he reached the bed, Eadric sat down, and Brandun reached out and placed his hands on his uncle's chest. The solid reality of Eadric's warm body and the vivid texture of his clothing filled Brandun with joy and relief. He leaned his head against the broad chest and breathed, "You're still here!"

Eadric's laughter echoed in his chest against Brandun's ear, and he clasped his nephew in a tight embrace. "Of course I'm still here!" he assured him.

"I've failed, Eadric," Brandun told him. "I can't go

on. There's nothing — it's not worth it..." His throat tightened, and he was afraid he would cry.

"Brandun," Eadric whispered, holding him against his chest. "All things are carefully watched and planned. There are no mistakes that can't be turned to good. Did it ever occur to you that things happen the way they do so that lessons are learned, by you and others? Did it ever occur to you that your errors might allow someone else's strengths to shine?"

"Eadric..."

"You are not alone, Brandun," Eadric said soothingly. "You are never, ever alone." Eadric repeated this last phrase over and over, and each time Brandun felt hope and love flow into him, strengthening him, and drawing him up.

Then Brandun's eyelids fluttered open, and he was staring up at branches stirred by a brisk breeze, and glimpses of the sky lit by morning. The river flowed by with a peaceful, rushing noise, and the forest sang with the morning twitter of birds. Brandun vaguely felt the ache in his body from lying tied up on the ground all night, but he seemed to be floating above it, buoyed up by the powerful feeling of hope from the dream. "I am not alone," he said softly. "I am never, ever alone."

Someone nearby moaned and shifted in his sleep. Brandun looked over and saw Thearl and his men still sprawled on the ground. Fitch was sitting against a tree, dozing, and Kempe was huddled on his side, still tied at the wrists and ankles. As the moans and shifting noises of the sleeping men grew more frequent, Fitch forced his eyes opened, yawning and stretching grumpily. Thearl sat up, then groaned and rubbed his head.

"You," he snapped, slapping the man next to him in the side. "Fetch some bread and ale. We must start pursuing Larke as soon as possible." The man rose and stumbled sleepily toward the saddle bags. Kempe rolled onto his back, heaved a deep sigh, and opened his eyes.

"My lord Thearl," Fitch spoke up. "Perhaps it would be best to let the girl go. You have the princes, and can surely gain the scepter and the throne. There must be some other girl who could satisfy your desires. She's not worth the time and effort..."

"Quiet!" Thearl snarled. "This is not just about desires. I have *chosen* Larke! She is strong, and will do well to bear *my* sons, and attend to me and my home." He stepped closer to Fitch, and spoke in a confiding voice. "A noble wife might be proud, and might not always obey me. A villein wife will know her place. And," he continued, his voice rising again, "I'll not be made a fool of! I'll find Larke and show her and everyone else that I'll *always* get what I want. Besides," Thearl added, relaxing his face into a grin, "she intrigues me. There's a fire in her that makes for a fine challenge. I think I'll actually *enjoy* this hunt we're about to have." Thearl wolfed down his bread and ale and then stood up, brushing the dirt from his clothes.

"There's another reason it would be wise to get Larke back," he told Fitch. "She provides good leverage for bargaining with our princes. They seem to care about her, and might be more willing to show us the way to the

91

Temple of Wisdom if we threaten her." Brandun's anger started to churn. His aches and pains had grown more vivid, and he felt his worry for Larke's safety returning.

"Fitch," Thearl ordered as he walked toward his horse. "You stay and guard the prisoners. I don't think this will take very long."

"Why me?" Fitch burst out.

Thearl glared at him and walked back toward him. "With all the luxuries I provide for you," he growled, inches from Fitch's face, "I expect obedience without question. I could reduce you to servant or peasant in a moment." Thearl swung around and strode to where the other three men were saddling the horses. They took off with a clatter of hooves along the packed earth of the river bank. Fitch watched them go, fuming with suppressed rage.

After a request from Kempe, Fitch untied them, one at a time, long enough to relieve themselves while their captor pointed a large sword at them. Then they were tied up again. Brandun winced as Fitch maliciously pulled the ropes tightly around his chafed wrists and ankles. After Fitch had begrudgingly poured some ale into each of their mouths, he threw over some bread, and they set to work once again to eat without hands.

Fitch went to rummage in his saddle bag for more food. As Brandun chewed a mouthful of hard bread, he noticed they had been tied up closer than before to the tree Fitch had slept against, and that Fitch's knife lay on the far side of the trunk. He looked at Kempe, and saw that he had noticed the same thing. While Fitch rummaged, muttering complaints about what little food had been left for him, Kempe sucked in his breath and rolled quietly toward the knife. Brandun's heart pounded as he watched Kempe roll once, twice. Kempe was within one roll of the knife when Fitch abruptly threw down the saddle bag and turned toward them.

Brandun yelled out in alarm, and Kempe froze. "Fools!" Fitch screamed. "Idiots!" He ran over and set his foot heavily on Kempe's chest, pinning him to the ground. The large sword he held was pointed at Kempe's throat. "Thearl takes advantage of my dependence on him," he shrieked, "and now you take advantage of my fatigue! How can I have all my wits about me when I've been up all night? I must have dropped my knife there when I dozed this morning." He bent over and snatched the knife off the ground, then hurled it angrily away.

"You tempt me to have an 'accident'," Fitch threatened, swinging the sword menacingly to his right. "I long to release my anger on someone. One prince could lead us to the Temple of Wisdom as well as two!" He raised the sword upward.

Brandun watched, terrified and helpless, and was startled to see a cloaked figure suddenly rise out of the brush behind Fitch. Swiftly, with three giant steps, muffled by the rustling of leaves in the breeze, the figure approached Fitch's back, carrying a rock in its hands. In a flash, the figure raised the rock high and threw it forcefully at the back of Fitch's head. The rock hit Fitch with a terrible thud, and the impact jolted his whole body. He tightened at first, then his sword clattered to the ground, just missing Kempe's arm, and Fitch came crashing down onto Kempe. Brandun gasped, then jerked his head to look at the person who had done this. The hood of the cloak had fallen back to reveal Larke, her face pale, her trembling hands pressed against her mouth.

"Larke!" Brandun shouted hoarsely, then turned quickly back toward his trapped cousin. "Kempe!" he called frantically, "Are you all right?" Kempe's head and shoulders stuck out from under Fitch's limp, heavy body. He was struggling for breath, having had the wind knocked out of him, and his face was white with shock. After a few tense seconds, his breathing came easier, and he looked at Brandun and nodded, indicating he was, indeed, all right.

Brandun looked back at Larke, who still stared at Fitch, and the blood on the back of his head. She didn't look at Brandun when he called again to her, but only lowered her hands from her mouth enough to say in a shaky voice, "That was it, Brandun. My second dream."

Chapter 12

As Larke stood trembling and staring at Fitch, Brandun called out to her in a voice as calm and soothing as he could manage. "It's all right now," he assured her. "You've saved our lives! Now I need you to come here and cut my ropes."

Larke didn't take her eyes off Fitch. "Is he — still alive?" she asked in a strangled voice.

"Yes," Kempe called out weakly. "He's breathing, but quite unconscious."

"We have to get Kempe out from under him," Brandun urged. "Get the sword that fell out of his hand."

Larke walked gingerly around Fitch and picked up the fallen sword. Kneeling behind Brandun, she worked clumsily on his ropes until they snapped apart. Brandun sighed with relief, rubbing his wrists, while Larke worked on the rope around his ankles. As soon as he was free, Brandun leaped to his feet, despite his aches, and rushed to where Kempe lay pinned to the ground. Tense with fear that the large man might wake up, he threw himself at Fitch's heavy body, shoving and straining until finally it rolled off Kempe and onto the forest floor.

Brandun collapsed onto his knees, staring at his older

cousin. Kempe stared back at him, drawing in deep breaths. Larke appeared with the sword and sawed at Kempe's ropes until he, too, was free.

"We must leave immediately," said Kempe, struggling to his feet and giving a hand to help Larke. He and Brandun recovered their swords and daggers from where they lay beyond the campfire, and tossed Fitch's sword into the middle of the rushing river. Larke grabbed their saddle bags and quickly gathered the abundance of food Thearl and his men had packed. After that, she filled her empty ale bags with water by the riverside.

"Let's go!" Kempe called urgently. He had loosed their three horses and set Fitch's horse free, slapping its rump to drive it away. "I think our only hope is to cross the river," he continued. "Thearl and his men will be looking in all directions on this side, and they won't expect Larke to cross since the nearest bridge is a day's ride away. But let's walk downstream a little, and find a place where our hoof and footprints won't show so plainly going into the river."

They led the horses downstream on foot, until they found a place where the grasses reached almost to the water's edge. Brandun looked at the wide, rushing river. "Will the water be deeper than our horses can reach?" he asked Kempe.

"There's one way to find out," Kempe answered. He mounted Sherwynd and urged him forward into the river. The large horse's body sank quickly, until only its head was visible, with Kempe's head close behind. The two drifted a great deal west before Sherwynd finally scrambled up on the opposite bank. Kempe slid off the horse's back and cupped his hands to his mouth. "Send Larke next!" he shouted.

When Larke was midway between the river banks, the current swept her off her mount, and she clung desperately to its neck as the animal swam resolutely forward.

"Hang on, Larke!" Brandun yelled, dreading the thought of her being carried away by the current. Kempe waded out until the water was waist high, his arms outstretched. When Larke's horse began to climb the bank, Kempe caught Larke in his arms, and brought her to dry ground.

It was Brandun's turn, and his skin tingled with nervousness as he mounted. Sparke descended into the cold, rushing water, and Brandun leaned into the current, gripping tightly with his legs. The river roared in his ears, and the shore ahead seemed to pitch and sway as Sparke's legs struggled beneath him to move forward. Just as his legs and arms began to ache from hanging on in the cold water, he felt the horse hit solid ground, and Sparke struggled up from the weight of the river and stopped, heaving, on the bank.

Brandun slid off the wet animal and leaned for a moment against Sparke's side. "Well," Larke spoke up lightly, "I think we all needed a bath anyway."

Brandun laughed, and saw that Kempe was smiling, too. "All right," said Kempe. "Let's head away from the river, where we can't be spotted from the other side." The three remounted and galloped off, leaving the river behind them. When out of sight of its banks, they turned east, and traveled for the rest of the day.

Sitting on their cloaks at twilight, the three watched stars appear in the clear sky, and talked softly together. Their clothing had dried, and spreading the soggy food out on top of the saddle bags for a while made it useable again.

"I think I see what those two frightening dreams did for me," Larke reflected. "They prepared me. When the things that were predicted actually happened, I was afraid, but at the same time I felt a strange sort of calm, like I had been through it before, and I wasn't shocked by the whole event. I was able to think, and not lose my mind." She paused a moment, thinking. "I'm grateful for the warning," she added. "I think without it, I would have panicked when Thearl grabbed me. And it would have been much harder to gather the courage to attack Fitch if my other dream hadn't prepared me. It showed me, ahead of time, that I was the only one who could stop him."

Brandun wanted to tell Larke his own dream from the night before, though he felt cautious about relating it. The memory felt precious, and he didn't want to expose it unless it would be safe. He looked at Kempe's shadowed face, wondering what he would think. Finally Brandun shifted position and cleared his throat. "I had — an incredible dream last night," he said in a low voice. As he carefully related the dream, Larke's eyes shone, and her lips parted slightly in a smile of wonder. Kempe remained still in the shadows, and Brandun couldn't make out his face.

"Oh, Brandun," Larke breathed when he had finished. "That wasn't just a dream. King Eadric was with you last night!"

"It *felt* like he was," Brandun acknowledged, leaning toward her. "But if it was, where is he?"

"He's — in the place that people go when they die. I don't know where that is, but I know it's a real place. My mother has talked with *many* people who have been visited in dreams by people who died. They're still very alive, just somewhere else."

Brandun breathed in the wonder of this thought. It felt easy to believe while the memory of the dream still glowed warm within him. *Of course I'm still here!* Eadric had said. *You are never, ever alone.* "Do you believe it, Kempe –" he asked his cousin abruptly, "that people who die are still alive somewhere, and maybe not as far away as we think?"

Kempe had picked up a stick and was whittling intently. "How can I know anything about it?" he snapped. "I've had no dreams like the ones you two describe. And what should it matter to me now? I suppose I'll find out when I die, like everyone else. There's no way to prove the point either way."

Brandun was surprised and annoyed by Kempe's attitude. "It matters to me," he retorted, "whether Eadric is still alive somewhere or not. And I'd like to know whether I can be with him again someday. *I* happen to miss him!" He pulled his cloak tightly around himself and lay down with his back to Kempe, to hide the tears that sprang to his eyes. After a few moments he heard

Larke lie down, and then heard only the steady chorus of crickets, and the repetitious scraping of Kempe's knife. Finally, the scraping stopped, and Brandun heard Kempe settle himself onto the ground. The fire grew low, the darkness closed in, and he slipped into sleep.

Chapter 13

When Brandun awoke, Kempe was saddling the horses. Brandun lay awhile and watched, weighed down by an ache of loneliness. Larke stirred and stretched, then opened her hazel eyes and smiled at Brandun. She reached for a bag of water, took a drink, and offered it to him. He sat up and took it with a grateful smile, letting small, leisurely sips slide down and wet his throat.

"Kempe wants to get off early," Larke commented softly, so that Kempe wouldn't hear. She studied the older prince for a moment, and then, smiling, shook her head. "He is handsome," she went on in a whisper. "When I first met him, I hoped he was the dashing prince who would take me away from Thearl and keep me for his own. I do admire him, Brandun, but he's not for me. He certainly keeps his distance, doesn't he? And now he seems to think we're both crazy."

Brandun nodded. "He's hard to understand."

Larke reached for some bread and handed it to Brandun. "I feel like somehow he's in pain," she said as they ate.

Brandun furrowed his brow. Kempe in pain? Nothing ever seemed to bother Kempe. He looked at

101

Larke as she watched Kempe, and realized how relieved he felt to know she wasn't falling in love with his handsome older cousin. Her friendship warmed a spot in his lonely chest, and he hoped she could feel the same from him.

"Larke," he said, "that dream I had — it made me feel wonderful. But I also feel more lonely today than ever."

"You're like many others," Larke told him.

"What do you mean?"

"My mother says that sometimes people who are visited in a dream feel very happy, but then also very sad, because it's made them remember how much they miss that person."

Brandun nodded, swallowing his last bite of bread over a large lump that welled up in his throat. Larke, as if seeing his emotions, softly touched his shoulder.

The sound of Kempe's footsteps made them both turn their heads. "The horses are ready," he announced, "so if you've both eaten, we should leave."

The three mounted and pressed their horses into a trot toward the newly risen sun. By early afternoon they could make out the distant green mounds of the Jahaziel Mountains. The sight filled Brandun with a thrill of anticipation, though he didn't know what to expect when they arrived.

They pressed on for the rest of the day, saying little to each other, their focus on the mountains in front of them. When the sun sank low in the west behind them, they finally stopped for the night, and Brandun realized how tired and hungry he was. Collapsing onto the grass, he eagerly accepted the cheese Larke handed him.

"We'll reach the mountains tomorrow," Kempe told them, chewing on his own meal.

"I need to be reminded," said Brandun between bites, "of what Ladroc told us about the Jahaziel Mountains. I can't remember very well. It seems like years since he talked about them."

"It has been," Kempe confirmed. "I'm sure he and Eadric had planned to refresh our memories when the time came for our journey there, but things have not gone according to plans."

"No," Brandun agreed.

"I've heard that some have travelled into those mountains and never come back," Larke offered, "so most people are not eager to go there."

"Are you afraid?" Brandun asked her.

"Mmm, a little," she replied. "But not as afraid as I am of Thearl. Do you mean King Eadric never told you about the Mountains, even though he'd been there?"

"Ladroc said Eadric's time in the Mountains was so precious that he didn't want to speak lightly of it," Brandun explained. "He wanted to wait for the right time to tell us about it."

"Here's what I remember," Kempe began. "Ladroc told us that it's a mysterious place because things don't follow the usual laws of nature. Riches and knowledge can be found there, but there is also danger. There are good people — teachers — who can lead a person to great knowledge, but there are also wicked people, who try to trap the person in delusions. It's a place where all people and things eventually show their true nature to anyone whose eyes are opened to it."

A breeze picked up as the daylight faded, and an owl called in the distance. Brandun looked at the darkening mountains, and realized that they would encounter more there than a shining temple and a golden scepter. But what? A shudder ran through him, and an uneasy acknowledgement that they were facing something totally unknown.

"And do you know what any of that means?" he asked Kempe.

"No," Kempe admitted. "Eadric would have given us more details."

The three were quiet now, listening to the increasing sounds of the night, looking toward the dark silhouettes of the mountain range, thinking about tomorrow and what it might bring. Then, one by one, each wrapped a cloak around his or her body and lay down for one last sleep outside of the Jahaziel Mountains.

When Brandun opened his eyes in the morning, it was still dark, with just a hint of gray tinting the air. The first of the morning birds were starting to call. Near him was a dark figure, sitting up, and when Brandun had blinked the sleep from his eyes, he saw that it was Kempe. He sat up and stretched, and then Larke stirred and sighed.

Kempe addressed both of them in a low voice. "Tell me this, dream experts," he said. "For years I've had the same dream come to me, over and over. I am in a room, and there is a closed door. I know that beyond the door is something I long for, but I also know it's something I'm not allowed to have. So I stand there, wishing, but not going near the door. For years, the dream has been the same, until this morning. This morning, I dreamed that I stood looking at that same door, but this time I knew that whatever it was on the other side was gone now — " his voice dropped almost to a whisper, "and I didn't know if I could stand it."

Larke was lying now with her head propped up by one arm. "What have you been wanting for a long time," she asked gently, "but not allowed to have, and now it's too late?"

Kempe didn't answer. He turned his head away in thoughtful silence, his profile silhouetted in the slowly increasing glow of dawn.

The sunrise over the peaks of the Jahaziel Mountains shone pink with a few lingering clouds. The three companions rose, ate and drank, and gathered their things. Once the horses were saddled and ready, they stood looking at the range ahead, its sloping forests green and bright. Then it was time — time to ride ahead. With a deep breath Brandun mounted alongside the others. The horses plodded forward, and Brandun felt almost sure that the Mountains were calling, inviting them in.

Chapter 14

By midday, they had reached the nearest foothills, and the first actual mountain rose majestically before them. These were ancient mountains, covered with forest, rounded and peaceful. They approached the north end of this first mountain, which stretched on to the south as far as they could see.

Reaching the base of the mountain, they agreed to turn and circle upward around its north side, since this seemed the easiest route. The forest was not dense, leaving plenty of space and sunlight between the trees. As the horses plodded upward, Brandun noticed the summer breeze blowing colder, until he wished he was wearing the cloak that was bundled in his saddle bag. "Does anyone else feel cold?" he asked finally.

"Yes!" Larke responded.

"I've heard that high up on mountains, the air is colder," Kempe remarked. "But we've barely begun to climb this one."

Brandun had pulled up alongside Kempe in the lead. He saw something on the ground ahead, and strained his eyes to see if it truly was what it appeared to be. A few minutes later, the group halted at the edge

106

of an area in which each blade of grass was coated with a glistening layer of frost. Looking ahead again, Brandun saw that the frosted blades soon disappeared under a sprinkling of powdered snow, which grew denser and deeper as the mountain slope continued. "Snow," Larke said in soft amazement, "in the middle of summer."

"We saw no snow as we approached this mountain," Kempe protested. "It was forested all the way to the top." He dismounted and strode over to the powdered whiteness, then bent and touched it, as if to see if it were real. He scooped a small mound onto his hand, and walked slowly back to the others, holding it out toward them. "It's just as Ladroc told us," Kempe said. "The weather in the Jahaziel Mountains does not follow the laws of the changing seasons." He dropped the melting mound onto the ground and wiped his palm on his clothes. "I suggest we put on our cloaks."

As they rode on, with cloaks held tightly around them, the wind grew colder and the snow deeper. The branches of bushy evergreens and bare deciduous trees were clothed with layers of white, and the horses' breath came out in puffs of white steam.

"There's someone there," Kempe pointed out suddenly. Brandun looked where Kempe indicated and saw what at first appeared to be a mountain lion walking on its hind legs. Brandun quickly realized it was a man clothed in a lion skin, with the face of the animal drooping down over his own. The rest of the furry hide covered his shoulders and wrapped around his torso, and his legs and feet were bound with a dark bushy fur which Brandun guessed to be that of a bear.

"There's another," Brandun said, pointing to a second man who emerged from behind some trees, also dressed in furs. He trudged in the same direction as the first. The riders continued slowly forward, watching the fur-clad men, until Kempe spotted something else coming up the snowy slope ahead of them from the left. It proved to be a chariot of sorts, though it traveled on runners instead of wheels. It was pulled by two small horses with clipped tails that stuck up into the air. The rambunctious animals scrambled wildly along the slippery upgrade, while their driver hung onto the long reins and urged them loudly onward. Soon more chariots came into view, some with one rider, some with two or three. Brandun saw other fur-clad walkers, too, plodding through the snow. Most were far ahead of him and his companions, though one chariot came near enough for Brandon to see a carved shape of a dragon on the front with horns that projected forward.

"Hello!" Kempe called out to the two riders in the dragon chariot. They turned toward him and raised their hands in greeting, staring curiously before they turned back. All the chariots and walkers moved in the same direction. "We could catch up and ask where they're going," Kempe said, "but since we're going the same way, we may as well see for ourselves."

The people on foot looked up in mild surprise when the riders passed by. "You're new here," one commented. "You'll soon need to put on your animal skins — it gets painfully cold without them." Brandun nodded in polite agreement. "Are you coming to the Gathering?" the man inquired.

"Yes, if we may," answered Kempe.

"Good," said the man approvingly. "We're almost there."

Brandun looked ahead and saw nothing but trees and snowy ground, with chariots and walkers making their way across it. But then a crowd came into view, and all the travellers joined this crowd as they reached it. When Brandun and the others approached, they saw a large mound of snow in the midst of this gathering, higher than their heads. Several men were digging intently at its base with thick sections of tree bark. When finally they hit something solid, other men with evergreen branches swept the snow away from the area to reveal two narrow doors side by side. The rest of the fur-clad people let out a cheer.

"It's a building!" Larke exclaimed.

The men struggled to pull the doors open, and the crowd filed eagerly in out of the cold. Brandun and his companions dismounted and followed the group of fur-clad people. Brandun could see the entrance, beyond the many heads in front of him. The room within looked dark, with only a few faint spots of light that looked like flickering candle flames. He squinted his eyes, peering ahead curiously, and had almost reached the entrance when a strong hand grasped his arm from the side, sending a startled jolt through his body.

"Wait," ordered a gruff voice. Brandun turned to see a tall man who was apparently guarding the door.

"Wait," he repeated, "you can't go in." He looked behind Brandun at the others who were with him. "None of you can."

"Why not?" Brandun asked, taken aback. The man turned back to Brandun and stared at him, his eyes narrow and almost fierce beneath the face of the lion's pelt that drooped low on his forehead. He didn't speak for several seconds, but only scrutinized Brandun's face with an intensity that made the young prince uneasy. The man's gaze was searching, yet confused, as if he were trying to discover something, but couldn't quite do it. Finally he glanced back at the others and spoke.

"You don't belong here," he said abruptly.

"We're searching for the Temple of Wisdom..." Kempe began.

"You don't belong here," the man repeated, agitation in his voice. "I can see it in your faces. You're some of those foolish enough to think they can understand the mysteries."

"What mysteries?" Brandun asked.

The man grew more upset. "The mysteries! The vast mysteries of God and life and death! Here at our Gatherings, our leaders tell us how we must have faith, we must believe and obey, but that we must never hope to understand these things. We do not want your kind here, and the questions you will bring!" The man's face burned red with agitation. Breathing heavily, he scowled and then turned to tromp away from them into the snow-covered building. Brandun caught one last glimpse of the dark room and the flickering candlelight before the heavy doors slammed in his face.

For a few moments, the three stood in stunned silence. The big man's words ran over and over in Brandun's mind. One phrase in particular stood out, and he spoke it out loud.

"Never hope to understand these things?"

"So strange," Larke murmured, "the way he stared into our faces."

"Let's go," said Kempe, turning abruptly toward the horses.

Brandun trudged behind his older cousin, shaking his head. *He can't tell me not to try and understand about death, and where Eadric is now,* he thought. *And what about God? I want to know where God is, and why He didn't rescue Larke and Aeldra from Thearl and Bardaric.* They reached the horses, who kept trying to shake the unexpected snow from their hooves. Brandun reached up to stroke Sparke's mane, and the gray animal turned to nudge his master, blowing clouds of white steam from his nostrils.

"Where do all those people come from?" Larke wondered, gazing at all the other horses and chariots that stood waiting for their owners. "Do you think these are some of the people that have gone to the Jahaziel Mountains and never come back?"

Kempe nodded. "I think that's likely," he agreed. "They may have come and settled here because they're comfortable with the way things are on this mountain."

"I could *never* be comfortable here," Brandun declared. "Their way of thinking would make life cold and dead, like this foolish snow that's turning my toes numb." He kicked at the snow, sending up a spray of white powder.

Kempe laughed derisively. "I don't think it's all *that* bad, little cousin," he said. "Not everyone feels the burning need to understand *everything*, like you do."

Brandun turned toward Kempe, his emotions rising. "All right then," he said, "*you* tell me. Why *shouldn't* I try to understand things?"

"There are just some things that a person *can't* understand, and doesn't need to. I don't understand Larke's dreams, but why do I need to? They're part of her life, not mine. And why should I struggle to understand things I can't see, like a life after death, and — God?"

"Because," Brandun retorted, his face growing hot, "not trying to understand about Larke's dreams might mean you don't care much about her. And having no concern about where Eadric is or whether you'll ever see him again might mean you never really cared about *him*."

The small smile disappeared from Kempe's face, and his look became as cold as ice. "How dare you say I didn't care about Eadric," he whispered.

"Please," Larke begged, stepping between them. "We're all tired and upset. Maybe if we got away from this snow..."

"You," Kempe continued, glaring at Brandun, "who have always been loved and cared for by Eadric and Aeldra, in a place that I could never enter..."

"They love you, too!" Brandun objected.

Kempe stepped closer to his younger cousin, and his voice trembled. "When our fathers died," he said with quiet anger, "I was older than you — old enough to have the pain dig deeper. My father was my hero, and I adored him. When he died, a huge hole was left inside of me. *Your* hole wasn't as deep as mine, because you were younger. And *you* were allowed to have your hole filled by a loving man who became a new father to you."

"Eadric wanted *you* as a son too!" Brandun insisted. "You never let him close to you!"

"It would have broken my mother's heart!" Kempe shouted. "Defena blamed Eadric for my father's death, and she made sure, year after year, that I would *not* forget my father, and that I would do *everything* in my power to be what he would have wanted me to be. I was not allowed to replace him with *anybody*." Kempe's arms went limp, and his voice dropped almost to a whisper. "I needed a father. And now it's too late." Brandun stared at him in astonishment. He had never seen Kempe like this. He never knew.

Larke hesitantly placed a hand on Kempe's arm. "Last night, you dreamed about a closed door," she said softly. "It was a bonding with Eadric on the other side — the thing you longed for but weren't allowed to have."

Kempe turned and walked to his horse. "Let's get out of this cold place," he murmured.

Brandun climbed onto his horse, and watched Kempe climb onto his. For the first time, his handsome, confident older cousin was sitting slumped in his saddle. As he rode forward, with Kempe ahead of him and Larke behind, Brandun replayed in his mind his life with

Kempe. He looked at all of Kempe's behavior, which had seemed so cold and distant, as the behavior of someone lonely and hurting. And as he did so, the lump of coldness he had felt toward his cousin began to melt.

Chapter 15

The riders continued around the north end of the mountain until they could see the next one rising up ahead of them. They descended, thinking they might do better to search a different mountain. As they traveled, the snow became thinner and the air warmer, until summer surrounded them once again. No one spoke, each immersed in his or her own thoughts. Brandun kept his eyes on Kempe, wishing he could express to Kempe what was in his heart, but words seemed clumsy.

A few weeks ago, life had been so simple. It seemed to Brandun like a distant childhood he could barely remember. Now the man who had been his father was dead, and he himself had been rushed off on a quest while still stunned by this loss, with many questions gnawing at the wounds of his grief. Aeldra and Larke were both in great danger, and he didn't know if he could help them. And seeing Kempe in this new way filled him with confusion and regret. What should he do, or say?

Larke passed food to everyone, and they ate on horseback. They descended little by little, approaching a valley as the sky became overcast with a dull, lifeless gray. A murmuring of faraway voices drifted up from beyond some trees, growing louder as they descended. Finally Brandun could make out some words from a few piercing shouts.

"Oh, how learned!" called a voice that faintly reached his ears, and another echoed the same phrase.

"Did you hear that?" Brandun asked the others.

"Yes," answered Kempe, straightening in his saddle. "Perhaps someone down there can give us some direction." As the ground grew more level, the trees gave way to shrubs, interspersed with nasty looking thorns and nettles. Here, many cottages lay scattered over the terrain, and in an area which seemed to be a town square, a large number of people stood packed together, shouting and cheering. The sound of their voices mingled with a dull, thundering noise.

"I don't like this place," Larke protested.

"Maybe someone here can direct us to the Temple," Brandun reasoned.

They approached the noisy crowd, dismounting at the edge of it. To Brandun's surprise, the people in the crowd were not only shouting and cheering, but stamping their feet, and the dull thundering noise that it caused rumbled up from the vibrating earth. "They'll wear a hollow in the ground!" Larke exclaimed.

Brandun could hear cries of "Oh, how learned!" amid the deafening noise. *Learned people might have answers to my questions*, Brandun thought. He had to find out.

"I see people on a platform in front," he said urgently. "I want to find out what they can tell us. Do you think we can push our way closer?"

"Let's tie our horses to these shrubs," Kempe suggested. "Perhaps if we link hands we can manage to get to the front together." Larke looked apprehensive, but agreed.

The three of them joined hands, and Brandun in his eagerness took the lead. Weaving and pushing their way through the sea of bodies, Brandun had his toes crushed more than once by a stamping foot before they finally approached the front of the crowd. The people they pushed past were caught up in the noise and excitement, and took little notice of them.

"See, Larke? There!" Brandun yelled.

He pointed over the few rows of heads left in front of them toward a line of men, handsome and elegantly dressed, standing on a platform facing the crowd. With new energy, Brandun gripped Larke's hand and eagerly pushed through the remaining rows of people until the three of them stood in front of a carved stone platform and stared up into the faces of the men who were the center of attention. The distinguished looking men smiled with pleasure at the enthusiastic shouts of praise from their audience. Their robes of deep blue hung to the ground, and the silver chains and pendants around their necks shone in spite of the overcast sky. A few feet behind them, another blue-robed man sat at a table, ready with pen, paper, and ink.

A man from the front row leaped lightly onto the platform and raised his hands for silence. Gradually, the shouting and stamping lessened, until finally the crowd stood quiet, waiting.

"Thank you all for coming," the man began loudly. "I know many of you have traveled far. You have come to hear these honorable, learned men, who have spent their lives pondering life's deepest questions. I now turn your attention to their scholarly words." The man stepped down off the platform, and one of the blue-robed men lifted his arms and smiled.

"Ask about any subject you please," he called to the crowd, "and we will try to give you a satisfactory answer."

A dozen questions leaped to the forefront of Brandun's mind. But should he ask them? He was just a visitor here, and hadn't been invited. Still pondering this, he was startled to hear Larke suddenly shout out a question.

"Should a man have the right to force a woman to be his wife?"

The speaker gazed down at her and smiled. "A very good question, young lady," he began, "but one that must be divided into several questions. First of all, does marriage really mean anything? Second, can we choose our lot in life, or is it decided by fate? Third, are there really human rights, and who can say what they are? And finally, can any person have power over another, or is it only an appearance? What do you think, my friends?" he asked the other blue-robed men. "Would it not take weeks, or maybe months, to come to a conclusion?"

The other men agreed, and the man at the table wrote on his page.

"We will write down your question, and discuss it

when we have time," the speaker told Larke with a patronizing smile. He looked over the crowd for the next question.

Larke furrowed her brow. "He certainly made the question more complicated," she muttered to Brandun.

Brandun struggled in his mind. The speaker's words sounded intelligent, but did they really have to consider all those things? Were there no simple answers to big questions?

Big questions. Before he could think whether to do it or not, Brandun called out, "Where is God when we need Him?"

"Ah," the blue-robed man responded, "a very big question indeed. To discuss this question, we would again have to divide it into several parts. First of all, is there a God at all? It may take *years* to come to any conclusion about that question."

The crowd murmured in agreement, and Brandun's stomach churned. Once again people were saying that the answers couldn't be found. As the speaker babbled on about how many issues they would have to discuss before they even begin to consider this question, Brandun sighed with frustration and closed his eyes. Hopelessness engulfed him, and he sent a silent message to a God he didn't know.

Help me understand.

Suddenly, something was different. Brandun snapped his eyes open, and his gaze was drawn to the eastern sky. There, the dull, gray haze was rolling away to expose a white circle of light. As the circle grew bigger, the light shot down in beams, enveloping the blue-robed men in whiteness. Brandun gasped as the light melted away the blue robes and silver chains, leaving the men clothed in black sackcloth and heavy, lead neck chains. Their handsome faces darkened to a dusky gray. Brandun looked wildly about him, but no one acted as if they saw anything unusual. Was he losing his mind? Beyond the crowd and the speakers, the houses, too, had changed in the light. They now appeared as broken down hovels, not fit to live in.

Brandun swallowed and faced the men on the platform again. A feeling of calm swept through him, and he realized the white light was shining not only onto those men, but into his mind. He was seeing them as they truly were. *It is a place where things and people eventually show their true nature, to anyone whose eyes are opened to see it,* Ladroc had told them. The light was making everything clear.

Suddenly, Larke gasped and clapped a hand to her mouth. "Brandun!" she choked out. "Look at them!"

"You see it too?" he asked eagerly.

She nodded, staring in wonder. Beyond her, Kempe also stared in shocked amazement, and then stepped boldly forward. "Who are you?" he demanded. "We hoped you could tell us where to find the Temple of Wisdom."

"Why search for something," the speaker asked, his voice cold and gravelly, "when we don't know if it exists?"

"You are all fools!" Brandun shouted, the white light

blazing in his mind. "You talk and talk, but you go nowhere! We'll learn nothing here." Kempe signalled that they ought to leave, and the three of them turned and walked away along the front edge of the crowd. After a few steps, Brandun felt the sting of a stone grazing off his arm. Turning, he saw that the gray-faced men had leaped to the ground and were picking up stones to throw at them.

"Run!" Brandun yelled, and they sped, dodging stones, around the outside of the assembly. Angry shouts started up from the crowd as many of its members scrounged for rocks and joined the speakers in flinging them at the three companions. Panting, Brandun dashed toward Sparke, and felt the blow of one more rock against his back before he and his friends reached the horses. After fumbling to untie the reins, they mounted and headed away from the noisy crowd. Brandun glanced once more toward the platform. The speaker and his companions had stepped back onto it, and to Brandun's surprise, they now looked perfectly still and gray, like statues of stone. The roaring crowd continued to hurl rocks, but didn't pursue them, not wanting to leave the speakers to whom they looked for guidance.

As the sounds of shouting and stamping feet faded into the distance, the riders slowed their horses to a walk. "That was amazing!" Larke burst out. "The white light completely changed those men, and it seemed that the people watching didn't even notice."

"I don't think they did," said Kempe.

"I asked for help — to understand —," said Brandun, "and then the white light came."

Kempe looked back. "So, did the white light show us the true nature of those men? That's what Ladroc said can happen in the Jahaziel Mountains."

"I think it did," Brandun responded.

"Their true nature," Larke pondered. "It was all so strange. Their faces looked like stone."

A little of the white light still fluttered behind Brandun's eyes. He felt it was trying to tell him things that he couldn't quite grasp. He tried to relax his mind, and then finally caught hold of one thought. "I think I see," he began hesitantly. "A statue has no life — it can't grow and progress. And a person can't grow and progress with many questions but no answers."

"Oh," Larke interjected. "Remember when you yelled at them, saying that they talk and talk and go nowhere? It occurred to me then that the stamping of the people was just like that — they were moving their feet, but going nowhere."

"The white light showed you that," said Brandun, and Larke smiled.

"Is this an exclusive friendship you two have with the white light?" Kempe inquired. "I didn't notice it telling *me* anything."

"Just quiet your mind and listen," Brandun urged.

Kempe turned to gaze back at the people that had grown tiny behind them, but were still visible. After a moment, a small smile tugged at the corner of his mouth.

"Their clothes turned black," he said, "because their words keep people in the dark."

Brandun grinned. "I think this white light would like to show us many things."

The horses picked their way through the shrubs, thorns, and nettles, and wound around and between the broken-down hovels. The sky remained overcast with a gray haze. Soon there were no more huts, and finally they reached the first trees which announced the next mountain, and the ground began to slope upward.

"Now," said Brandun, relieved to be leaving that gloomy valley, "let's hope this mountain holds better luck for us!"

Chapter 16

The upward slope of the next mountain drew them out of the valley. Soon a thin forest surrounded them, and the gray haze above broke and gave way to brilliant blue. To the west, the sun approached the horizon, and the faint beginnings of sunset colors, lavender and orange, glowed softly beneath it.

Brandun inhaled deeply, taking in the pure scent of pine and grass. The horses climbed until they reached a piece of ground that was reasonably level.

"Let's spend the night here," Kempe suggested. "The horses will be able to stand comfortably."

After dismounting and unpacking cloaks and food, the three companions hunted for firewood. A friendly blaze was crackling by the time the sun had sunk from view. As they ate, they chatted quietly about the valley.

"Do you think," Brandun asked, "all those people in the crowd were trapped there, as Ladroc said can happen? They didn't try to follow us."

"It seemed that way," Kempe agreed. "Perhaps if we had believed what the speakers were saying, we would now be trapped as well."

"Stamping our feet, but going nowhere," Larke added,

poking a stick into the fire. "I think sometimes you just need to believe in something because it makes sense, even if you don't have it completely figured out yet."

"Yes," Brandun agreed. "I think that's right."

He pictured again the white light that had shown him the truth when he was confused. It was definitely alive. It had seen him, and heard his thoughts. It had cared about what he needed.

"I wonder if it's God," Brandun said softly. "The white light, I mean."

Larke stopped poking her stick and looked at him. "It certainly had great power," she responded.

Brandun stared into the fire. "Eadric and Aeldra would hold services in the castle chapel sometimes, and pray," he remembered. "They taught me that God was Creator and King of all. I pictured Him on a throne somewhere up in the sky, looking down to see how things were turning out." He began to feel dizzy from the movement of the flames, and realized how tired he was. Pulling his cloak around him, he lay down, and Larke did the same. Kempe remained sitting awhile, silent, then settled himself onto the ground near Brandun.

Brandun ached to know what Kempe was thinking, ached to say something meaningful after what he had learned about his older cousin on the snowy mountain. But all he could manage was a simple, "Good night."

"Good night," Kempe answered.

Many thoughts swam through Brandun's mind, but exhaustion finally won, and he sank into a blissful, relaxing sleep. Dreams came to him, of riding Sparke at full gallop, leaping effortlessly over logs and boulders. He dreamed of looking up at the sun, basking in its warmth and light, and of dipping his hands into cool, flowing water that refreshed his whole being. Then the dreams changed.

Everything was spectacularly vivid. He could make out every leaf on a towering tree he stood beneath, and could feel the tickle of grass under his feet. He could sense his heart beating, and hear his breath as it accompanied the rustle of leaves in a breeze. The earth smelled rich and fruitful, and into this dream walked a person. It took barely a moment for Brandun to recognize him, to feel the rush of joy, and to run full speed toward him.

"Eadric!"

Barreling into his uncle's broad chest, he threw his arms around Eadric's living, breathing body, and felt the wonderful laughter shake him once again.

"You've come back!" Brandun exclaimed.

"You would be amazed," Eadric told him, clapping him on the back, "how close I stay to you."

Brandun looked up into Eadric's face. It was undoubtedly Eadric's, but the skin was smooth, the hair and beard a dark chestnut brown.

"You're young!" Brandun commented in surprise, and Eadric laughed heartily.

"Of course," he responded. "No one remains old here."

Brandun looked into Eadric's blue-green eyes as, without words, the two continued to communicate. Thoughts flew from one mind to another, conveying messages much more quickly and fully than words ever could. Eadric told of the place where he now lived, in the world after death, where *real* life began, and everything made sense.

How can I be here now? Brandun wondered. Eadric explained that every person's spirit exists in both worlds simultaneously, but that only after death would the eyes of his spirit fully open to this spiritual world, and stay open. Until then, one might have glimpses now and then, but no more.

Brandun told of Kempe's pain, and of his need for Eadric. Eadric assured him that he was staying near Kempe as well, especially since Kempe had fully realized his need for a closeness between them. *I'll be with Kempe tonight, too,* Eadric communicated with a smile.

Brandun sensed their visit coming to an end, and clung tighter to Eadric. Eadric took Brandun's face in his hands and spoke. "Yes, Brandun," he said gently, "our visit must end for now. Since you still live in the physical world, we cannot speak like this for long. But I am with you every time you think of me." Brandun felt strength flow into him from Eadric's hands. His panic quieted, and he nodded.

"Before you go," Eadric went on, "I want you to look over there." He pointed toward a field of flowers, where a man and a woman stood in the distance. Brandun couldn't make out their faces, but as he looked at them, he felt a new love expanding in his chest. The love was coming from them.

Who are they? Brandun wondered, and Eadric answered his thought.

Your mother and father. You cannot see them clearly, because you do not know them now. But they know and love you, and have watched you grow. You will know them one day.

The scene faded, and Brandun found himself staring up into a night sky filled with stars, his face wet with tears. He sighed deeply and didn't move, trying to hang on to the feeling of the dream. Crickets sang in soft rhythm, and the wind whispered soothingly.

A choking sob startled Brandun. Kempe rolled onto his side and cried, his arm covering his head. Still filled with emotion from his dream, Brandun sat up and pulled himself over to his cousin. He laid his head on Kempe's shoulder and put his arms around him, letting him cry. Kempe's body shook with sorrow, and when finally he calmed himself, Brandun asked, "Were you with Eadric?"

Kempe turned his head sharply to look at Brandun, amazement in his eyes. "How did you know?" he questioned hoarsely.

"I was with him, too," Brandun answered.

The two of them sat up and looked at each other.

"It was so clear — the dream," Kempe began. "It felt real."

"It was real," Brandun insisted.

Kempe nodded. "He — loves me," he continued, pausing to swallow. "He said he understands why I've been distant, and that it doesn't matter. We can start over, he and I."

Brandun smiled broadly, swelling with happiness for his cousin.

"There was more," Kempe added. He gazed to the east where a faint golden glow signalled the onset of dawn. "There was my father." He smiled, and his eyes glistened.

"Your father!" Brandun repeated happily.

Kempe turned slowly back toward Brandun. "My father is proud of me," he told him. "He says to follow my own path, wherever my heart tells me to go. Nothing I choose, as long as I choose be for good purposes, will disappoint him." He turned his head back toward the east, where the edge of a glowing, orange sphere crept over the horizon, pushing back the night.

"I'm sad for the time I could have been close to Eadric, and wasn't," Kempe continued. "But I feel hope, because the time to be with him is not over — it will never be over." He looked back at Brandun. "I see now why it was important for you to know if people still live after death."

Brandun nodded. They were quiet, watching the dawn, when Larke began to move and stretch. She smiled before opening her eyes — a smile full of peace and contentment. "Oh," she said when she saw Brandun and Kempe awake. "It was wonderful. I was with my grandmother, sitting on her lap like I used to do. I had forgotten!" She sat up and smoothed her hair. "My grandmother died six years ago."

Brandun quickly told her of his dream, and Kempe did the same. They talked excitedly, sharing the wonder and amazement of what had happened.

"How can it happen," Brandun wondered, "that we all have such incredible dream visits on the same night?"

"It's this place!" Larke replied, standing and stretching the sleep out of her body. "The Jahaziel Mountains! Here we're closer to the world where my grandmother and your fathers all live. I think it must be easier for them to speak to us here."

Brandun suddenly felt eager to continue their search for the Temple of Wisdom. "Let's go," he said springing up.

"After some food, little cousin," Kempe said with a laugh, and the term that had always been said with derision was now filled with warmth. Brandun didn't mind being a "little cousin" now.

While they ate Brandun wanted to ask Kempe more about his dream, but Kempe seemed immersed in thought, and not eager for more talk. Brandun remembered his own feelings after his first dream encounter with Eadric — the joy, and then the lonely ache. Remembering, too, how good it had felt when Larke reached out and touched him during that time, he laid a hand on Kempe's arm. The blue-green eyes of the older prince turned toward him and softened. "It's nice to know they are alive," he remarked, "but it's hard to live in separate worlds."

A lump swelled in Brandun's throat, and he nodded. They finished their bread in silence, and then Kempe stood, brushing the crumbs from his hands. "Let's go," he suggested.

130

Chapter 17

When the ground became steeper, the companions led their horses on foot. The calls of birds sounded from tree branches, welcoming the warmth of the new day. Brandun gazed at the vivid blue sky, feeling full of vigor and enthusiasm.

But when the sun had reached its peak, they were still wandering the mountain, with nothing in sight but more trees, grass, shrubs, and an occasional animal or bird.

"Stop!" Brandun called out finally to Kempe, who was in the lead. "Let's sit awhile. I'm thirsty." They tethered the horses, who promptly began cropping anything green within their reach.

Brandun fished a waterskin out of his pack and flopped to the ground with it. After a hearty drink, he passed it along and began pulling at the leaves on a shrub next to him.

"There's nothing here," he said, trying to control the frustration in his voice. "There are so many mountains. How are we supposed to know which one to look on? This could take weeks."

Kempe sighed and loosened his belt. "We *can't*

know," he answered. "I had hoped it would be more obvious than this."

"It's only our second day here," Larke pointed out, but then put her hand to her mouth, ashamed. "Oh, I'm sorry," she said. "I'm just so glad to be out of Thearl's reach, I'm forgetting the Queen, and that you must get back to her, soon!"

Brandun thought about Aeldra and Lord Bardaric. Abruptly, he stood up and began pacing. "Maybe we should go back. Maybe we can find a way to get rid of Lord Bardaric, and then we'll come back to these mountains when Aeldra's safe. Maybe Ladroc could tell us more about the Jahaziel range, and give us some guidance."

"You're forgetting that it was Ladroc who insisted we leave right away, in order to do something about Lord Bardaric," Kempe reminded him. "We don't know how many allies Bardaric has, or how many tricks he'll try. And it was Eadric himself who was worried about not having an heir established. It leaves too much room for confusion."

"All right, all right," Brandun replied, his aggravation growing. "You're always right, aren't you?"

"No," Kempe responded. "But I am this time."

"Then which way shall we go?" Brandun demanded.

"Now *that* I don't know," Kempe shouted.

"Never mind," Larke interrupted, raising her hands to quiet them. "Let's rest here a while and calm down. We're just tired and confused."

Brandun sat down, ashamed of his outburst. "I'm sorry," he mumbled to Kempe.

"It's all right," Kempe replied.

They sat in silence, frustration tainting the air. Brandun felt angry — angry at himself, angry at Lord Bardaric, angry at Eadric for dying before he could tell them what they needed to know.

But at the thought of Eadric, his uncle's face came into his mind, with a look so loving Brandun's throat ached and his anger melted. Eadric hadn't chosen when to die. So who did decide to take him away at that moment? The concept of God as a distant ruler came into Brandun's mind, immediately followed by the image of the White Light, which had heard his thoughts, and had helped him to see. He suddenly felt tired, too drained by confusion to be angry at God. If that Light was God, it wanted him to see.

"I'm just worried," Brandun said aloud to his friends, "that we're going the wrong way. What if we're travelling away from the Temple, instead of toward it? What if our mistakes are wasting precious time, while Aeldra is in real danger?"

Kempe shook his head slowly. "I don't know, Brandun," he responded. "I wonder the same things."

Brandun scanned the woods around them, despair weighing him down. There were so many directions they could go. *What do we do?* he asked from his heart. *Please show us what to do.*

No beam of light came from the sky, revealing the path that they should follow. But a small, gentle sound, distinct among the rustlings of the forest, made them all turn toward it.

There, between two trees, surrounded by a faint golden glow, stood a beautiful woman. Her silken gown was white, but hints of rainbows glistened in the folds. Her hair cascaded to her waist, warm with shades of brown and gold. One arm was extended, reaching toward them, and she spoke a single word.

"Trust."

The word was spoken softly, but it resounded in Brandun's soul with great power. He had asked what they should do, and she had told them. As the three companions stared, transfixed, the woman gazed into each of their faces. Her own face was calm and loving, with a hint of a smile which seemed to say that she knew them, and that she knew everything would be fine.

Gracefully, the woman lowered her arm and spoke again. "Your journey is taking you toward the Temple of Wisdom," she assured them, her voice soothing and musical. "Our loving God is guiding your every step, yet there are things you must go through before you are ready to find the Temple. Continue travelling, and whatever happens, remember what I have told you. Do what you must do, and trust."

And with a shimmering, she was gone. Stunned, Brandun stared at the now empty space between the two trees.

"Oh, I wish she'd come back," Larke burst out, startling him out of his trance. "The way she looked at me! I felt so — comforted."

Brandun looked at Kempe, who slowly turned his eyes away from the place the woman had stood. "I don't know where she came from," Kempe began, returning Brandun's gaze, "but she's told us what to do. Go forward, and trust."

Brandun smiled, his energy restored.

Chapter 18

It took until midday to descend the mountain, sometimes riding, sometimes leading the horses. The next mountain rose green and majestic to the east, across a misty valley.

"Valleys haven't proven to be good places, so far," Larke commented, eyeing the land below them.

"True," Kempe agreed. "But we can't get to the next mountain any other way."

As they reached the first wisps of mist on foot, Brandun heard a faint rumbling and raised his hand for the others to stop. "What's that?" he asked intently. The three of them froze, listening.

"Horses, galloping," Kempe deduced. They fixed their eyes toward the sound echoing from the north curve of the mountain. From around the curve, about a quarter mile away, several figures on horseback came riding rapidly toward them. Larke's breath quickened, and she cried out in fear.

"Thearl!"

Grabbing desperately at her horse's saddle, she scrambled onto the animal's back. Brandun and Kempe mounted immediately, just in time to follow Larke as she dug her heels into the horse's flanks and shot downward into the mist. The wispy mist quickly thickened into a gray-white fog, limiting their range of vision and blocking Thearl from view as the threesome galloped recklessly forward. Larke was close to panic, and Brandun and Kempe fought desperately to stay near her.

"Got to hide!" Larke screamed to them. "He'll keep following!"

But where could three people and three horses hide? The valley seemed to be a barren plain, with nothing more than patchy grasses and shrubs that passed under the horses' pounding hoofs. Brandun felt close to panic himself.

"Follow me!" Kempe shouted at him, and it was an order. Kempe leaned forward onto Sherwynd's neck, driving the big horse harder until it caught up with Larke's horse.

"Follow me!" he shouted at Larke, repeating it several times until she acknowledged him with a nod. Driving his horse past Larke's, Kempe led them through the fog. Minutes seemed like hours as they thundered along, and Brandun could feel sweat on Sparke's straining neck.

Quite suddenly, a large shadow appeared in the fog ahead of them, and within seconds it materialized into a building. Kempe veered to the left around it, while Brandun and Larke, startled by his sudden turn, pulled vehemently on their horses' reins to swerve after him. On the back side of the building, Kempe slowed his mount and leaped off, keeping hold of the reins. "Get off! Get off!" he yelled.

Brandun slid off, nearly falling as he landed. Regaining his balance, he clambered after Kempe, pulling Sparke by the reins.

"Send the horses off," Kempe ordered. "They'll be a decoy." He slapped Sherwynd's flanks and shouted, and the others did the same. The horses, skittish and frightened by the commotion, whinnied and took off in a wild gallop.

"Let's hide inside," Kempe urged, breathing hard. Brandun looked at the building beside them and saw it was built of reeds, with many chinks and spaces in the walls where the mist oozed through. Making their way swiftly around the structure, they found openings in the east wall large enough to crawl through.

"He's coming," Larke whimpered, and plunged through one of the openings. The others followed as thundering hoofbeats and shouts drew near. Just inside the wall of reeds hung a dusty cloth, and the three companions, not expecting such an obstacle, floundered against the cloth, stepping on it and becoming entangled. Finally they wrapped the ends around themselves and huddled together in stillness. Brandun held his breath as Thearl and his men clattered past.

When the shouts and hoofbeats had faded, Kempe let out a loud sigh of relief. Brandun was astonished at Kempe's ability to think and act so quickly in a crisis. It was truly a strength that he himself didn't have.

"Thearl may be back," Kempe pointed out. "Shall we leave and take our chances in the mist, or see if there is a good place to hide in here for a while?"

"Wait," Larke whispered abruptly, laying a hand on each prince to silence them. "I heard something moving — behind us." Brandun's skin crawled as he, too, heard a soft rustling. They were not alone in this building. Someone was waiting behind the curtain they leaned against. He swallowed and looked at his companions, who stared back at him in worried silence. It was Brandun who was on the end and could most easily peer into the room behind them. He shuddered at the idea, but braced himself to do it. Slowly he turned his body and, taking gentle hold of the curtain, leaned his head to let one eye peer around the edge.

Brandun jolted at the sight that met his eyes, bumping into Larke. A row of eerie, round faces, tinted with a pale, reddish hue, glared at him menacingly. These faces were attached to bodies in dark, hooded cloaks which sat on a long wooden bench. They sat facing away from Brandun and the curtain, but had turned to look at him.

"What are you doing!" one hissed harshly. "What business have you coming through the east wall? Come in, and close that curtain!"

Brandun swallowed and shakily walked forward, with the others close behind. The menacing faces followed them, scowling, until the threesome had crossed in front of the bench and stood before them. On the west wall was a large door, the only door in the building. Mist poured in through chinks in the west, south, and north walls, swirling lazily around the room. Only the east wall was obscured with a heavy cloth. Two benches, one facing west and the other north, were filled with cloaked

139

figures. In front of each person stood a small table, upon which were open purses, full of gold coins which overflowed into gleaming piles on the table tops. The eerie, round faces had relaxed a bit, now that the companions stood before them. All of their eyes glittered with a strange insane light.

"Give us your gold," the same one hissed.

"Who owns all of *this* gold?" Kempe asked sharply. His tone surprised Brandun. The younger prince looked over to see his cousin staring intensely at the gold, as if captivated by the sight. Larke, too, was looking from table to table, her eyes blinking rapidly.

The air vibrated as all of the figures drew in a breath and spoke in unison. "I do!" they chanted. "The gold is mine!"

Brandun was startled by the outburst, and watched them glare at each other, as if wishing to grab each other's gold, but no one reached for another's pile. He looked again at the purses and shining coins, and as the mist swirled around him, he felt a force draw near, then enter his body. It was like a dark hand, reaching into his soul and groping for something. Finally, it found what it was looking for, and Brandun felt it latch onto a dark corner of his mind, pulling it forth. Memories came to him, of wanting things that weren't his — longing for Kempe's sword when he was a child; aching to have the first horse Kempe was given, the saddle with silver trim, the dagger with a jeweled hilt. With each memory came flooding the desperate emotions of wanting; the conviction that if only he could have that thing, could possess it for his own, he would be happy. Now those emotions rushed together and focused on the gold in front of him, and though a tiny voice of reason reminded him that he had plenty of wealth available in his life, desire for those shiny coins grew like an approaching storm cloud. So much gold in one room! What one could do with so much wealth!

Suddenly, a loud thud behind him broke the spell. Brandun and his friends whirled around. The door swung open, and in a cloud of gray mist, Lord Thearl strode into the room. Larke gasped. Instinctively, Brandun and Kempe drew closer together and pushed Larke behind them. Thearl looked at them, grinning triumphantly, and laughed.

"My men have surrounded the building," he informed them. "Your little decoy had us going for a bit, but your horses were too loyal. They soon slowed down and turned to look for their masters. We thought you may have snuck in here." Thearl took a step forward, then noticed the gold on the tables and stopped. Slowly sweeping his eyes around the room, he took in the sight with an expression of amazement. The pupils of his eyes began to glitter.

"Whose gold is this?" he asked.

"It is mine," the cloaked figures chanted in hushed hisses. "The gold is mine."

"No," said Thearl, his voice growing raspier. "It is *mine*." Brandun felt sick, realizing that in Thearl's eyes he was seeing the emotions that had just been taking over his own mind. Thearl fired his gaze at Larke.

141

"And *you* are mine! Obey me!" The insane light in his eyes grew more intense.

Behind him, Brandun could feel Larke's terror. The three of them slowly backed away from Thearl, but the tall lord followed.

Suddenly, Larke turned and bolted around the bench filled with cloaked figures. She dashed to the east wall, grabbed hold of the curtain and yanked the heavy cloth aside. White light flooded the room with vibrant, radiant rays. Cries of anguish went up from all the cloaked figures, because where their piles of gold had sat were now tiny piles of dust. Thearl's cry was loudest of all. He ran crazily from one table to another, searching for the gold, and shouting accusations at the cloaked figures. Roughly, he grabbed them one by one, searching beneath their dark garments while they wailed in protest.

"Come," Larke urged, pulling at her friends. "Thearl is distracted! Let's run!"

Kempe drew his sword. "We'll have his men to contend with," he reminded them, and pushed himself back through the chinks in the east wall, disappearing into the powerful light. Brandun drew his own sword, and also his dagger, which he handed to Larke. Taking her arm, he followed Kempe.

Outside, Brandun met the full brilliance of the White Light, and was shocked to feel a sudden impact to his chest which knocked away his breath and weakened his knees. He released Larke's arm, struggling to keep his footing, and then realized what it was. In the presence of the all-seeing Light, he was overwhelmed with shame at the emotions he had felt in the reed hut. That dark force had reached into *him* and found an ugly greediness. He stumbled forward, wishing to hide or to die, to somehow escape the knowledge that perhaps he was no better than those hissing creatures in the hut, or than Thearl himself.

A strong hand grasped his arm and shook him. "Focus, Brandun!" Kempe said sharply. "Thearl's men are approaching!" He released Brandun and leaped forward to meet the first attacker. The clang of metal as their swords met jolted Brandun fully into the present. Fear for Kempe and for Larke shot energy back into his limbs. He pushed Larke behind him just as a second man raced from another side of the building, rushing at Brandun with a drawn sword. Brandun braced himself, jaws locked in determination, then dodged to one side as the man made his first thrust. In the seconds it took for the man to regain his stance, Brandun felt a fleeting rush of dark fears, wanting to weaken him — the man was bigger than he, they were outnumbered, he himself was a wicked person.

"No!" Brandun burst out. He had no time for those fears. He and his friends were in danger. And as he pushed those dark fears aside, he felt a new force enter him, a force of Light. It strengthened his limbs and sharpened his mind. He met his opponent's next attack with all the skill he had ever learned battling Kempe in swordplay, taught by Eadric's best soldiers. He struck and dodged and blocked, compensating for his smaller size with greater agility. Never before had Brandun fought like this, and his fear gave way to a thrill at the Power that filled him.

143

From the corner of his eye Brandun could see that Kempe had managed to knock down his opponent and was now dealing with a third man who had arrived. Larke was nowhere to be seen. Then Thearl emerged from the reed building, scowling. He eyed the two sword fights, then scanned the area for something else.

"Larke!" he roared.

Beyond the clang of swords and the grunts of fighters came a new sound, a thundering of hooves. Out of the mist and into the circle of Light that bathed them came Larke astride her own tawny horse, clutching the reins of Sparke and Sherwynd who galloped on either side of her. Without slowing down, she barreled into the midst of the fighting, sending Kempe and his opponent sprawling.

Brandun's assailant glanced fearfully at the oncoming horses, and poised himself to run. Brandun leaped at the man, threw his arms around him, hooked his foot around the man's ankle, and tackled him to the ground. In a moment, the thundering hooves were upon them, and the man screamed as the three horses leaped over them, the treacherous hooves missing them by inches.

As soon as the horses were past, Brandun pushed up, and before his enemy could collect himself, broke into a run. Ahead of him, Larke slowed a bit to turn around for another run, but seeing Brandun, she released Sparke's reigns.

"Sparke!" Brandun yelled. The horse whinnied in reply and ran toward his master. Grasping the saddle, Brandun swung himself up, urging Sparke forward before he was fully seated. His enemy chased him, but Brandun veered to the side and escaped, heading back to help his friends.

Near the reed hut, Kempe still battled his opponent. Thearl tried to approach Larke, but she maneuvered her horse to stay out of his reach, brandishing the dagger with a trembling hand. Brandun galloped up, sword ready, and went at Kempe's adversary, freeing Kempe to run for Sherwynd and mount.

Kempe scrambled into his saddle. "Hurry!" he yelled hoarsely, leading the way. "They're going for their horses!" With a signal from Brandun's heels, Sparke bolted into the mist after the other two horses. Swirling grayness enveloped them, clouding their vision. Brandun could just see the back of Larke's horse, and heard behind him the shouts of their pursuers. On they rode, swerving this way and that to lose their enemies, keeping silent, trusting that the sound of their horses' hooves would be drowned out by the galloping of their enemies' own mounts.

Gradually, the shouts and curses of Thearl and his men grew more distant. The dark-haired lord was riding off in another direction. Brandun's breathing relaxed a little in relief, but at the same time he wondered, *Where to now?*

As if in answer to his wondering, a white glow appeared ahead. Brandun wanted to shout to the others, but stopped himself, knowing that Thearl might hear him. After several minutes of riding, the glow grew larger, and the mist thinner. He could now see not only

Larke's horse but Kempe's in front of hers. The ground began to slant upwards, and low trees came into view. Then, in a burst of glory, brilliant blue sky became visible, and they saw, swelling up before them, the forested slope of the next mountain.

Chapter 19

The riders continued swiftly up the mountainside through the thickening forest. Brandun's skin stung from several cuts and scrapes, and some bruises had begun to throb. But he saw, thankfully, that he had no serious wounds from the battle, and it appeared that Kempe was just as fortunate.

Soon the ground became steep, and they dismounted to lead the horses. An hour passed. It was well into the afternoon, and Brandun's stomach growled with hunger. When finally they came to a patch of level ground, he asked, "Do you think it's safe to stop and eat?"

Kempe paused and looked behind them. "I think it is," he concluded. "We've heard nothing behind us since we reached this mountain." They tethered the horses, then flopped to the ground, eagerly pulling food from the saddlebags.

"I don't care to go through that again," Larke said, clutching her bread and looking anxiously back toward the valley.

"I really think we've left them behind," Kempe assured her.

Brandun put a hand on her arm. "You were amazing," he said. "You could have run, but you brought our horses to us."

"Very courageous," Kempe agreed.

Larke blushed. "It was nothing, compared to what you two were going through." She poured a bit of water into her hand and washed a scrape on Kempe's knee where his leggings had torn. He winced, but allowed her to clean it.

Brandun took a bite of his bread and chewed thoughtfully. "The woman told us to trust. And we were taken care of. I felt power from the Light."

Kempe nodded. "It didn't take away our enemies," he said, "but it strengthened us."

"That strange hut," Larke commented, shaking her head, "and those strange people in it." She shuddered, and took a bite of her own bread. Brandun remembered, uneasily, the ugly feelings that rose inside of him in that hut.

"But you broke free of those feelings, Brandun."

The voice was soft, but very clear — soothing, musical. With a gasp, Brandun whirled around to see, once again, the beautiful woman they had met on the last mountain. Kempe and Larke dropped their food and stood up.

"You're back!" Larke exclaimed.

The woman laughed warmly at their surprise, a laugh full of kindness and love. "I come to wherever I am needed."

"Where do you come from?" Kempe asked her.

She looked in his eyes. "From the world after

death," she explained. "I and many others have a full life there, but are sent to your world when we are needed. Sometimes you see us when we are with you, but most times you do not."

"Here, in the Jahaziel Mountains," Larke began, "are we closer to your world than we are when outside the Mountains?"

The woman nodded, her shining hair fluttering gently in an other-worldly breeze that Brandun couldn't feel. "A special link has been established here," she explained, "and the walls between the worlds are thinner than they are outside the Mountains. When people come here seeking truth, they draw to themselves people and things from my world that can help them along. But over the years, those who have come here for selfish reasons have attracted people and things from the dark side of the world beyond death."

Brandun thought of the dark force that had reached into him in the reed shack, and his shame returned. The beautiful woman already knew what had happened within him down in that valley. She turned toward him again, gazing at him with kind eyes, inviting him to speak. His mouth went dry. Swallowing, he opened his mouth to try and say something, but Larke interrupted.

"I — learned something in that reed building," she began, looking uncomfortable. "I have always hated the way Thearl wants to possess things and people, and have control over all he can. But in there, I found myself wanting that gold, just like those horrible cloaked creatures, and remembering times when I had wanted things that I had no right to. Perhaps," she continued, looking down at her clasped hands, "I'm not much better than the man I'm running from."

Brandun felt a flood of relief at her confession, and embarrassment that she had been the first to admit it. "I felt the same thing, Larke," he blurted out.

"And I, too," added Kempe, sullenly.

"The forces of darkness present in that hut want you to think you're no better than Thearl," the woman responded, her voice soothing. "But when the White Light entered the hut, were you upset to have the gold disappear?"

Brandun and Larke looked at each other. "No," Larke answered for them and Kempe shook his head in agreement.

"So you see," the woman reasoned with a smile. "You have more in you that attracts the Light than the darkness. That is why the Light could fill you with power during your fight against Thearl's men. Every person has dark places within, places of selfishness. The more you know of them, the more you can reject them, and choose the Light instead. Thearl and those in the hut have not rejected the darkness, so it rules them. When the gold disappeared, Thearl continued to look for it."

Brandun's spirit lifted, and he smiled back at the woman. She lifted her hands toward them, and her dress shimmered with its hundreds of soft colors. "I will go now," she said.

"Wait," Brandun protested, not wanting her to leave. "Won't you please lead us to the Temple of Wisdom?"

The woman smiled gently, but shook her head. "Some places you must be led to from within yourself. But I'm permitted to tell you this much. It is here on this mountain." Then she began to sparkle, like sunlight on the water, and was gone.

After a moment of stunned silence, Brandun turned excitedly to his friends. "The Temple of Wisdom is here!" he exclaimed. "Our search is nearly ended!"

Chapter 20

The three of them sat down and earnestly discussed a plan.

"We'd cover more ground if we split up," Kempe reasoned.

"And what will the one who finds it first do?" Brandun questioned, feeling an unexpected rush of distrust toward his cousin. With their goal now so near, the old urgency was returning.

"The one who finds it first will then find the others and bring them to it," Kempe answered firmly, glaring at Brandun in annoyance.

"Of course," Larke intervened, shaking each one good-naturedly by the shoulder. "Let's each choose a direction and follow it."

Kempe looked around him. "This place is a small clearing," he noted, "and these rocks around the edge will help us recognize it again. We'll meet back here at dusk."

"Whether we find it or not," Larke added. "Whoever finds it will need to come back *here* to get the others."

Brandun looked at the sun, which was just beginning to sink toward the west. "We don't need to search west," he pointed out, "since we came from that way."

"Right," Kempe agreed. "I'll go north, Larke will search to the east, and you, Brandun, go south. Keep your eye on the sun, and try to go in a relatively straight line, so you can find your way back here."

Hastily they parted, each sure they would reach their destination soon.

Brandun hurried through the forest, feeling as though he was in a race. How could he possibly find the Temple before Kempe? Kempe was faster and more capable. Behind him, Sparke snorted in protest at being pulled so quickly through the brush. Brandun slowed down, realizing his foolishness. It wasn't supposed to matter who found it first. That person would then notify the others. Kempe wasn't so base that he would go back on that agreement.

Now plodding at a walk, weaving through rustling trees, Brandun recognized his true fear: that Kempe was more suited to be king than he was. And with that recognition, he saw how very much he himself wanted to be king. He thought of listening to people's problems and finding ways to help, as he had with Lufu back in Tamtun. The helping had been neither easy nor pleasant, but the satisfaction it produced and the bond with the people there had been wonderful.

He thought of the conversation he had overheard back at the inn, and his interest in exploring whether lords ought to have such power over the lives of their tenants. He thought of King Eadric with his people, listening, deciding, taking action.

But when it came to taking action, wasn't Kempe the

153

superior one? Wasn't he the quick thinker, full of confidence, a real leader? Brandun grabbed at leaves and twigs as he walked, flinging them down in frustration.

Time plodded on with his feet. The scene before him didn't change, no matter how far he walked. The trees seemed to go on forever. And when he stopped to catch his breath, he realized with exasperation that he hadn't been concentrating on traveling due south. He had been weaving around, following whatever path through the trees he could find. Light from the setting sun was behind him now. Using the sun as a guide, he was able to turn south again, but he didn't know how long ago he had veered away from his course. Every direction looked the same. He couldn't find the others if he wanted to.

Brandun leaned against Sparke and looked around. *It's no use,* he thought, sighing heavily. *It's getting dark, and I'm getting nowhere.* And probably, he added bitterly to himself, Kempe had already found the Temple.

Though he couldn't see the sinking sun, he could see the orange glow it cast into the forest, and it made him think of the White Light. Once before he had asked for help, and the Light had helped him to see. Would it work again?

Please, he asked earnestly with his eyes closed, *I don't know where to go, or what to look for. Would you help me find the way?*

He cracked his eyes open, then widened them in alarm. In the last glow of the orange light, a form was taking shape. It looked at first like a mass of dark mist, then a shadow. Finally, a person with hunched shoulders stood before him, as small as a child, but with the sagging, wrinkled face of a crotchety old man. This face was set in a sour pout, its eyes darting around until they met Brandun's.

"What?" the little man yelled, pointing a finger at Brandun. "You see me?"

"Who are you?" Brandun demanded, trembling.

The little man approached, twisting his mouth into a sour grin. "I'm a friend of yours," he said.

"Stay away," Brandun ordered, taking a step back.

"I'm a friend," the man continued in a whining voice, "who knows how unfair things are for you. Why should Kempe be the one who's taller and more handsome? Isn't that what people admire? It's not fair that he's better at fighting and battle plans. Aren't *you* better than *him* at talking to people, and listening? Wouldn't you know more about communicating with your subjects? *You* know what it takes to be king, Brandun. It's not fair!"

The pouting, twisted face drew nearer, and Brandun watched, mesmerized, shaking his head. He knew he had thought the things that the little man was saying many times, but hearing them aloud made him cringe. He didn't want to think them any more. He liked Kempe — no, loved him now! And this wrinkled creature wanted to ruin it!

"No," he protested. "Kempe would make a great king!"

Quick as lightening, the little man darted behind Brandun, and, before he could react, leaped onto his back. Brandun cried out in horror and flailed about, trying to shake the creature loose. The little man laughed gleefully and hung on, his nails digging into Brandun's flesh. "I am your friend!" it shrieked. "I will stay with you!"

"No," Brandun yelled fiercely. He sank to his knees in anguish, breathing heavily. "You are an idiot," he cried out. "I do not want your friendship!"

Just for a moment, his gaze was drawn to the distant orange light. A breeze hit his face and quickly grew to a gusting wind. *Yes,* he felt from the light. *Fight for what you truly want. You have the power of choice.* He felt his body absorb warmth from the orange glow, power flowing into the parts of him that wanted to be free of pouting and envy. With firm, deliberate movements, he reached back and grabbed the little man's clinging hands, pulling with all his might.

"Aaaah," the creature wailed. "You always let me hold on before!"

His muscles bulging with effort, Brandun tore the horrible hands from his shoulders, and with a yell threw the creature over his head onto the ground.   The wind howled, and the little man screamed, his face contorted with the fury of a child having a tantrum. Then he vanished in a dark, smoky mist. Trembling, Brandun sank to the ground as the wind quieted.

After some minutes had past, Brandun prayed again. Night had descended and all was dark, but somehow he felt that the Light was present. "Thank you," he said, though he didn't quite understand all that had happened.

"There's so much I don't know. I want be king, but maybe it's not meant to be."

The forest was silent now, except for a soft tinkling sound. "Water," Brandun uttered, realizing his thirst. He scrambled to his feet and fetched Sparke, who had shied into the brush during the struggle. Together they plodded forward, Brandun feeling his way through the dark, following the sound.

Soon a mountain stream was at his feet, and he gratefully flopped onto his belly and plunged his face into the cold rushing water. Beside him, Sparke also sucked in great gulps. When he had drunk his fill, Brandun pushed himself to a sitting position and wiped his face with his sleeve. But a sudden sound made him freeze — the sound of something rustling in the brush. Was there some other creature out there to plague him? Brandun sat silently, hoping it was a harmless animal, but to his dismay, Sparke suddenly let out a boisterous whinny. Instantly, the horse was answered by another whinny, and a voice called out, "Who's there?"

"Kempe?" Brandun yelled, leaping to his feet.

"Brandun?"

Brandun splashed across the stream, straining to see through the darkness. He followed Kempe's voice as they continued to call to each other. Soon they collided and gripped each other, laughing, in a hearty embrace.

"I've never been so glad to see anybody," said Brandun.

"Come here," said Kempe, putting an arm around

157

Brandun's shoulders. "I've found a spot clear enough to sleep in."

"What about Larke?" Brandun asked.

"We're lost, and have no chance of finding her in the dark," Kempe answered. "We'll have to trust that she's all right for now." When Kempe had led Brandun to the tiny clearing, and both were lying on their cloaks in the dark, Kempe told his story.

"I wanted so badly to find the Temple," he began. "But the trees went on and on, with no change and no trail. I had no plan to follow, and I realized how I had always gained strength from *knowing* something about the obstacles or enemies I faced. Using certain skills of search and conquest, I can be quick to form a plan, but here in this endless forest I had nothing to form a plan *with*. I know nothing about this Temple we're looking for. Will it be huge, in a clearing? Or hidden, in the forest? Will people live there? Should I look for signs of human life?

"I became tired and confused, wondering why I had suggested we split up. Had I hoped to be the one to find the Temple first? Did I want so much to be king? I thought about Eadric, his endless counsels and decisions and all the listening to the needs and disputes of his people. Eadric was a warm and caring ruler. Can I do that? Do I want to?

"I didn't know what I wanted, or what to do. And then I realized that I'd been so caught up in these thoughts I had changed direction without knowing it! I found myself walking east instead of north. Now I was lost, and that was just too much. I was so overwhelmed that I actually prayed out loud. I called out, asking where I should go, and why I was here. If the God of Light was nearby, I begged Him to show me the way. And then, an amazing thing happened. In the last orange light of the setting sun, a dark, misty form took shape."

Brandun's skin tingled as he remembered his own experience. He listened quietly.

"The shape seemed human, but there was something snake-like about it as well. I was frightened and drew my sword, yelling at it to stay where it was. It was startled, as if surprised that I could see it. Then like a smoky mist, it began to change shape, and in a moment I found myself staring at my mother!"

Brandun gasped.

"At first," Kempe continued, "I wondered if somehow, in these strange mountains, Defena could have been brought to me. It looked so much like her! Then she spoke. Her voice was gentle, but her words were hard. She asked why I had not yet found the Temple, reminding me of my duty to do honor to my father's memory. I tried to explain what my father had told me in a dream, but she wouldn't listen.

"She talked on, asking if I would disgrace myself by letting my younger cousin gain all the glory, and rule over me. I tried to protest that it wouldn't be a disgrace if you were chosen, but she interrupted again, accusing me of not having enough determination and strength to gain the prize of the golden scepter."

Kempe sighed. "It was hard, Brandun. I felt the

159

frustration of all the years since my father died, trying to please my mother and make her happy, even if what she wanted was hurtful to me. But soon I knew this couldn't be Defena. Despite her faults, she loves me, and has never spoken to me like this, interrupting and forcing her will on me, with a voice as cold as ice. I realized that this thing in the shape of Defena was speaking all the fears that hovered in my own head. I lifted my sword and cut her in half."

"What happened?" Brandun exclaimed.

"She changed back into mist, moved around a little, and then took a new form. King Eadric. This time, though, I was ready, and did not listen to his urging me to find the Temple first and become king, so that he and I could be connected in glory. I sliced through him as well.

"Then the mist formed itself into its true shape — a towering man with a puffed out chest and a laurel wreath on his head. I swung my sword through him as well, but he laughed at me. 'Your weapon cannot harm me,' he scoffed, 'but you are wrong to be fighting me, Kempe. I know you well, and I am on your side.'

"Then the thing gripped my hand, and his grip was too tight. He drew close, and whispered that he would help me. 'We will not let Brandun take the throne from us, as he stole Eadric's love,' he said. 'You are the warrior. You will conquer and take what is yours. Brandun is a child. You are a man.'"

Kempe sighed again, heavily. "His words were poisonous," he went on. "They called up familiar feelings of hurt and envy and pride. But I have newer feelings. Peace with Eadric, permission to follow my heart from my father, and — new respect for my younger cousin... ."

In the darkness, Brandun smiled.

"...so I knew that I had a choice. I had closed my eyes while the thing talked, but now I opened them. The last orange sunlight was almost gone, and darkness was all around. I don't remember being afraid of the dark before, but I was deathly afraid of this darkness. And my hand was growing numb under the grip of this thing.

"I yelled out to the orange light, crying that I didn't want this darkness. I wanted help. Then a wind blew up, and I felt this — this surge of heat or power within me. I turned all my strength on the creature, knocking it to the ground, pounding its arm with my free fist to make it let go of me. And though my sword had had no effect on this demon, it struggled beneath my fury, and finally let go of my hand. I held it by the throat while it changed back to Eadric and then Defena, trying to dissuade me. Then it shrank back to a dark, misty shape and disappeared, and I collapsed."

Brandun had been holding his breath, and now let it out with relief.

"After all that, I heard water," Kempe concluded, "and remembered how thirsty I was. I found the stream, drank, then lay on the ground until I heard Sparke's whinny." Kempe paused a moment, then laughed. "I don't know how to be king. I don't know if I *want* to be king — and I have no idea where we are. But the strange thing is, I think that it's all perfectly all right."

161

Perfectly all right. Yes, that described the feeling well, thought Brandun as they lay together in the dark forest, the sounds of the night surrounding them. "And now," said the younger prince, "*I* have a story to tell *you*." And he told it, while the water trickled musically beside them, and the horses dozed beneath the trees.

Chapter 21

Hope. Brandun felt it the moment he became aware of morning sunlight that coaxed his eyes to open. He blinked and stared until the branches above him came into focus, and then he sat up. What was it? He felt an excitement, as if something was about to happen. And at the same time, he felt an unmistakable assurance that Larke was all right. There was no logic behind this knowledge, and yet somehow he knew it, as certainly as he knew that the sun had risen that morning.

Carefully, he raised himself from beside his sleeping cousin and walked softly to the stream to drink. But the rushing waters invited him further, so he pulled off his clothing and stepped in. With a gasp, he sat down in the cold current that reached to his waist. When his lower half had somewhat adjusted to the frigid temperature, Brandun gritted his teeth and fell back, plunging his upper body and head into the stream. The icy water seized him, shocking his body fully awake. Quickly, he pushed himself back up and shook his head like a dog, gasping and laughing from the exhilaration of the plunge, and from the giddy feeling of hope and excitement with which he had awakened.

When Brandun opened his eyes, he saw Kempe grinning down at him, arms crossed. "A drastic thing to do to yourself, first thing in the morning," he commented.

"It's only for the brave," Brandun taunted through chattering teeth.

Rising to the challenge, Kempe stripped and threw himself in, face first, splashing Brandun heartily in the process.

"Refreshing," Kempe declared when he came up, his voice several notches higher than normal.

Brandun laughed and scrambled out, his skin tingling and clean. Kempe rolled about a little more before he emerged, his wet body glistening in the morning light that filtered through the trees. All seemed fresh and new and wonderful.

Brandun ran back to the spot where they had slept and pulled his cloak out of his saddlebag to dry himself. Reaching for the other bag, he pulled Kempe's out, too, and held it out as his cousin approached.

"What did you feel this morning, when you woke up?" Brandun asked.

Kempe paused from drying himself to look at Brandun intently. "A strong, amazing feeling that Larke is fine, and that today is wonderful," he replied. "I want to find out *why* it's wonderful."

"Then we must get going," Brandun insisted. Hastily they tugged their clothing back on and loaded the saddles and bags onto the horses. Brandun felt a vague grumble of hunger, but it seemed of no importance next to the urgent feeling to move on and see what lay ahead.

"The feeling's getting stronger," Brandun declared. He felt a definite pull to go in one certain direction. "That way," he said, pointing, and Kempe nodded. Taking hold of the horses' bridles, they plunged through the thick foliage, weaving urgently among the trees along the stream, until they saw the edge of the forest. There, Larke sat by the water, gazing away from them at the amazing sight that burst into view as Brandun and Kempe emerged breathlessly into the sunlight.

It was a building, the likes of which Brandun had never seen, nor ever thought possible. It rose to a great height, and its four walls were each perfect squares. These walls were of clear, sparkling crystal, vibrantly reflecting the rays of the morning sun. The roof was gracefully arched, formed of transparent jasper. A flight of steps, gleaming white, led to an arched door at the front, and the building was surrounded by a garden of lush green trees.

"It has to be," Brandun marvelled. "What else could it be?"

Kempe nodded. "The Temple of Wisdom."

They walked over to Larke, and she greeted them with a beaming smile. "Isn't it stunning?" she asked them happily. "I found it before the sun went down, but a voice that spoke right into my mind told me not to go back to the clearing. It said to stay here, because you two were being led here as well."

Kempe and Brandun looked at each other, then back at Larke. Brandun took her hand, and raised her to her feet. Together, the three of them walked, transfixed, away from the woods and toward the shining building. But just as Brandun felt ready to break into a run, Kempe grabbed his arm. "Listen," he warned.

Brandun held still and caught the sound of horses blowing air through their lips. But it was not their horses. To their right, before they could react, Thearl and two of his men emerged on horseback from the forest, not twenty paces away. With his face locked in a snarl, Thearl fixed his glare on the three of them, drew his sword, and approached, moving to position himself in front the princes and the girl. His henchmen did the same. Brandun's throat went dry, and he drew his sword in answer, as did Kempe. The ringing scrape of both blades being pulled out of their sheaths sounded almost in unison. Larke was behind them, silent, but Brandun could feel the vibrations of her fear. *Thearl had three men with him in the valley*, thought Brandun, glancing around anxiously for the third.

When Thearl was five paces away he stopped, right between the three companions and the spectacular Temple. Panic brewed in Brandun's chest. Thearl was now closer to the Temple, and on horseback! He could easily turn and reach their destination before them. Could he take the scepter by force and carry out his plan? Would the people of Haefen take it as a sign and accept him as king?

Thearl's mount was breathing heavily from carrying its master up the mountain slope, but Thearl breathed heavily, also, as did his men. The dark-haired lord labored to catch his breath and speak. "Curse this moun-

166

tain air," he spat out angrily. "It makes my head dizzy. But our swords outnumber yours, even though Kempe's weapon left one of my men lying dead in the valley." He paused for breath again, then pointed his sword furiously and continued through clenched teeth. "Princes," he hissed, "I will let nothing stop me. You will lead me to the Temple of Wisdom now, or you and the girl will die, one by one."

Lead him to the Temple? When it was right behind him? Brandun opened his mouth in utter confusion, and burst out, "Lead you to the Temple?"

"Yes, fool!" Thearl bellowed, urging his horse forward. The point of his sword drew closer to Brandun's face. "Now! Or I will cut right through you to that vixen wench and cut her in half as well!"

Brandun felt Kempe move in closer. But rage rose within him at the mention of harming Larke, and her safety became the essential thing. "Who's the fool," he shouted back, "when you bother with *us* while your prize sits right behind you?"

Thearl jerked his horse around and looked directly toward the glittering Temple. Then he spun back again in anger.

"Stinking vermin!" he shrieked, gasping for breath. "You think childish tricks can deceive us? There is nothing there, and now you die!"

Like bellowing bulls, the three riders attacked. Brandun braced himself, while his mind whirled with bewilderment. Nothing there! Thearl saw nothing there!

Moving aside to avoid Thearl's sword, Brandun was

167

knocked down by the horse of one of his henchmen. Grunting as he hit the ground, he rolled, then scrambled back to his feet as Thearl turned his horse and came at him again. He was vaguely aware of Kempe engaged with another rider, and of the third chasing Larke toward the trees. But the sight of the dark-haired lord riding at him, eyes filled with rage, his chest heaving as he struggled to breath, made him suddenly feel all alone against his enemy. His heart filled with fear, and his mind went numb. Somehow his body assumed a position of defense, sword raised to block Thearl's.

All of life seemed to slow down. Thearl came, his eyes locked with Brandun's, his mouth open and panting, his arm raising his deadly sword up higher, and higher. And suddenly, it was upon him. Thearl's heavy sword swung down while Brandun's launched up, and they met in a deafening clang. Brandun knotted every muscle in his body, used every ounce of strength within him, and to his great surprise, his sword held! Through the pressure of their locked weapons he realized that Thearl's strength was not full, that whatever was causing him to struggle for breath had also weakened him considerably.

But Thearl still had the uphand advantage, and Brandun fought against gravity as well as Thearl's remaining strength. Sweat seeped from his skin. His arms began to shake. Then, with a mighty effort, Brandun arched his body beneath the clashed swords and scraped his weapon out from under Thearl's. The snarling lord had been leaning forward too far. He toppled forward with a cry, flailing his arms and sword out in front of him to catch his fall. But as his blade hit the ground, its deadly edge was up, ready to meet Thearl's throat. In an instant, he had crashed down upon it, and was dead.

Brandun sank to his knees, exhausted, and looked desperately toward the trees for some sign of Larke. To his great relief, she emerged from the woods, looking pale but unharmed, and ran toward him. Turning in another direction, Brandun saw Kempe walking slowly away from one of Thearl's men, who lay on the ground, unmoving.

Brandun glanced back at Thearl. Blood had begun to seep out from under the fallen lord's body. Brandun covered his face with his hands and collapsed.

Chapter 22

Gentle fingers pulled Brandun's hands from his eyes, and there before him was the Temple of Wisdom, as radiant as before, silently calling him forward. The same gentle fingers now touched his face, and he looked up into the anxious, hazel eyes of Larke.

"Are you hurt?" she questioned, and he shook his head no. Kempe came and flopped onto his knees beside him.

"The one I battled is dead," Kempe informed him, then paused to catch his breath. "Something was strange — he was weak, and breathing hard. It didn't take much to defeat him."

Brandun pushed himself up to a sitting position. "And what about the one that chased you into the woods?" he asked Larke.

Larke shook her head. "I don't understand what happened. I wove through the trees, trying to lose him. I could hear him behind me, panting and wheezing. Then, it seems, he ran into a tree branch, and was knocked off his horse. I heard him fall, and then he didn't move. I didn't want to look too closely, for fear it was a trick, so I ran back here."

Brandun looked toward the woods. "He must be

170

dead or unconscious, or else he would have come out by now." The man's horse stepped leisurely out of the woods and began cropping grass.

"It's over for now," said Kempe, and they turned back toward the Temple. The three of them stared at the glowing, transparent building, and then, one by one, each rose silently and started toward it. The closer they came, the quicker their paces became, and they were almost running when they reached the garden of trees that surrounded the structure.

The garden was made up of four different types of trees, each with its own distinct leaves and graceful beauty. They paused by an olive tree, its bark covered with intricate grooves, its branches laden with plump olives. Larke laid a hand on its trunk.

"These are wonderful," she said. "This garden is deeply peaceful."

They were now near the gleaming white steps, which were made from polished alabaster. Alabaster figures of lions with their cubs, majestic and protective, graced either side of the steps. Large precious stones in striking colors studded the foundation of the building, forming a row around its base. Brandun reached down to touch the steps. They were smooth, cool, and solid.

"Thearl couldn't see it," he marveled, confused, but his chest swelled at this awesome sight.

Brandun looked at Kempe, who laid a hand on his shoulder and squeezed gently. "Our search is finished," Kempe declared softly, and Brandun knew it was true. A deep contentment within him told him beyond a doubt.

He turned to see if Larke was ready to go in, but Larke shook her head. "I don't feel I'm supposed to enter," she explained. "This is a special time for you two — it's what you came for."

Brandun felt unsure for a moment, but Kempe pressed him forward, and together the nephews of King Eadric climbed the alabaster steps. At the top, they passed through an arched doorway cut out of the crystal wall, and stepped onto a floor of smooth cedar wood, glowing golden in the light.

The Light. The Light was everywhere. It poured in through the crystal walls in brilliant rays, and through the jasper ceiling in soft, radiant beams. There was nothing in the room but the Light, and yet there was no intense heat — only a beautiful, loving warmth that filled Brandun's soul.

For a moment, Brandun caught a glimpse above him of beautiful, winged figures, flying beneath the ceiling, but they vanished when he looked straight at them. Love. Light. It enveloped him, and made him almost giddy with delight. There was a shimmering in front of him, and a beautiful man appeared.

The man, too, was golden and full of light, though Brandun could sense he wasn't *the* Light. His hair, his eyes, and his long garment were golden, and he exuded goodness and love so tangible Brandun could feel it like rays of warmth. This man, Brandun sensed, would never have an unkind thought, and accepted others joyfully for what they were. The man smiled, and his radiance brightened.

"Kempe and Brandun," he greeted. "I welcome you from my heart. I have watched your journey, and watched the Light guide you to this place. Thearl and his men found it hard to breathe because the atmosphere here does not agree with them. Their spirits are in conflict with the Light, and they cannot function in a place where God's love is so purely felt."

"Why couldn't Thearl see the Temple of Wisdom?" Brandun blurted out.

"Because," the golden man explained, "it can only be seen by someone who acknowledges that everything they know is but a drop in the ocean compared to what they do not yet know."

Brandun remembered his feelings in the forest the night before, after his struggles with the repulsive little man. "Do you mean," he asked hesitantly, "it is a good thing to realize how little you know?"

"It is essential," the man replied earnestly. "Anyone who, like Thearl, thinks himself as wise as he needs to be has closed his mind. He is not open to learning from others, or to realizing that all knowledge and intelligence ultimately comes from the One Teacher, our God. But those who see their own knowledge as barely anything have minds that are open to the Light, just as this Temple is. And this, nephews of Eadric, is the beginning of wisdom."

"The beginning of wisdom?" Kempe repeated.

"Yes," the golden man responded. "Wisdom is much more than knowledge and intelligence. Wisdom is learning for the sake of living a good life. And wisdom must

173

be joined with love and usefulness to become whole. It is these three things together that make a person an instrument of the Light.

"Thearl's mind was closed," Brandun murmured, marveling, "so he couldn't see this amazing sight."

"It is the Light *inside* your mind which enables you to see the Temple of Wisdom," the man explained. "It is amazing how many things a closed mind cannot see. You must work to keep your minds open, nephews of Eadric. Beware of ever thinking that you know enough. Keep the walls of your mind transparent and receptive."

"When one of us becomes wise," Kempe asked, "will he then be fit to rule Haefen?"

The golden man smiled. "Wisdom is not a destination, but an ongoing journey, taking you ever higher. You must have a certain amount of knowledge to begin the task of ruling a kingdom, but you certainly cannot know all. The important thing you have shown by finding this Temple is that you are willing to keep on learning. This makes each of you worthy to be heir to the throne of Haefen. And yet, there is to be only one king."

The man held his hands out in front of him. Several beams of lights, streaming through the walls and roof, came together in his hands. There a glowing shape began to form, blazing like fire, then lengthening and smoothing into fine gold. The man held up the elegant object for them to see — a golden scepter, with a golden horse carved at its head. Brandun caught his breath and stiffened, realizing that the moment was here. And did he not still hope what he had hoped before?

"Both are worthy," the man continued, "yet one is chosen. But is the one chosen more valuable than the other? No. Every position, every occupation, every job, is an essential part of the whole. Every human being is chosen as a particular part of that whole, chosen to perform a particular service. Your loves, your talents, and all your experiences in life lead you to that position of usefulness. This scepter is given to the one chosen to serve his kingdom as king. And this scepter, Brandun, is for you."

At first the words didn't sink in. The golden man reached forward, offering the glittering scepter, and slowly Brandun lifted his hands to receive it. The metal felt warmed by the all encompassing light, and Brandun felt a thrilling rush as he took it in his grasp. He stared at it in wonder.

"Me?" he whispered.

"A horse symbolizes the understanding of truth," the man told him, "because, as a horse carries a man on a journey, an understanding of truth carries your mind along the journey of life. You, Brandun, are gifted with a strong desire to understand truth, and since this scepter is given here, in the Temple of Wisdom, it is bonded to your spirit. It is a symbol of the king you will be, and of your specific strengths. Let the golden horse remind you to ever pursue a deeper understanding, of people and of truth. You will be a great and effective ruler, if you continue to grow in wisdom."

"How shall I do that?" Brandun asked.

"Search for truth in the books of religion," the golden man directed. "Learn about people and their needs by listening to them. Take counsel from people who are skilled in areas that you are not, and who have experience that you do not have. Take action as best you can, and learn from your mistakes. Push away the darker forces in yourself that may block the Light."

The darker forces in myself. "Is that what happened last night in the forest — the awful little man that clung to me?"

"Yes," the man affirmed. "Both of you asked for help from our God, the Light, so you were shown the dark forces that were keeping you from finding this Temple. Dark spirits cling to all people, unseen, but once you recognize them, they are weakened, and you can resist them."

The responsibility that the scepter represented was large indeed, yet, bathed in the Light, Brandun felt only joy. He was filled with a confidence that the Light would give him the ability to be king.

Suddenly, Brandun became aware again of Kempe's presence beside him, and his joy was replaced by a sick feeling in his stomach. How could he be so selfish? What was Kempe thinking at this moment? Brandun was ashamed, and afraid to look at his older cousin. He hung his head, not knowing what to do. But the silken voice of the golden man began again.

"Kempe," the man said softly. "What have you come here wanting?"

Kempe was silent a moment. Brandun looked hesitantly up at his face and saw that it was calm.

"I thought I wanted to be king," Kempe began. "But along this journey, I've realized that I wanted it in order to please others. My mother wants me to be king. Many expect it of me because I am the older nephew. And I thought that my father wanted it, too, but he came to me in a dream and set me free. I do not want to be king. I find excitement and challenge in battle plans, defense tactics, and outwitting the enemy. A king must focus mainly on the lives of his subjects, and listen to their problems. I hope I can become better at helping people, but Brandun is more suited to that than I am." He looked at Brandun meaningfully. "I'll gladly call him king, and serve him."

Brandun blushed and looked down at his scepter.

"You do help people, Kempe," the golden man assured him with a smile, "but in your own way. Your loves and skills are better suited for captain of the king's army, and if you, too, continue to grow in wisdom, you can be the greatest that Haefen ever had."

Brandun looked at Kempe and spoke with gratitude. "I'll always listen to your counsel in matters that involve the army, or keeping order in the kingdom — or rescues," he added with a grin, remembering the way he had bungled Larke's rescue. Kempe grinned back.

"Your friend awaits you outside," the golden man declared, stepping back from them, "and Haefen awaits you. Go in peace, and remember the Light." In a shimmering, he was gone, leaving the princes alone in the brilliance that flowed into the Temple of Wisdom.

"This incredible Light," Kempe marvelled. "It seems alive!"

"It is alive," said Brandun. "It is God." It made sense now, that this place was called a temple. A temple is a place of worship.

To acknowledge that all good is from God, and to let in the Light, is to worship God, came a thought from the rays.

And will You stay with me when I leave this place? Brandun wondered.

Yes, always, came the emphatic reply.

Chapter 23

It was hard to leave the feeling of love that pervaded the Temple of Wisdom, but finally Brandun and Kempe turned together and walked across the cedar floor to the door. Descending the alabaster steps, they looked around until they spotted Larke resting under an olive tree. Seeing them, she leaped to her feet and approached them eagerly.

"Oh!" she gasped when Brandun showed her the glittering scepter, then shot a worried glance at Kempe.

"There's nothing to worry about," Kempe assured her with a peaceful smile. "Everything is just right."

"Truly?" Larke asked happily. She threw her arms around Kempe, laughing with relief, then turned and locked Brandun in a joyful embrace.

"We have so much to tell you," Brandun began, "about what happened inside."

"And I'm more than eager to hear it all," said Larke. "But you can take your time. We have the whole journey home to spend together."

Brandun looked over at Kempe, meeting his eyes. Kempe's face expressed what Brandun had always longed for from his older cousin — brotherly affection, and respect.

179

"I really am relieved," Kempe reassured him. "All that I told the man in the Temple is true. I don't know what Defena will say, but I know my father — and Eadric — approve."

"And I meant what *I* said," Brandun responded. "I'll learn from the mistake that Eadric made with our fathers. Things are peaceful in Haefen now, but if ever there's trouble, I'll always let you have the final decision in battle."

Kempe got down on one knee, a playful smile on his face. "Well, then, sire," he said, "I hereby pledge my allegiance to you."

"Don't," Brandun protested, blushing. "I'm not king yet!"

Kempe laughed, and Larke joined in. Larke darted between the princes as Kempe stood up and linked arms with each. "Can I wait until we're out of the Jahaziel Mountains to treat you as a king?" she asked Brandun. "Right now, I want to treat you as my friend."

"Of course," Brandun answered, flustered. "Will becoming king mean I have to give up my friends?" They laughed some more and started away from the Temple.

Beyond the garden of trees, they saw Thearl and one of his men lying on the ground. All three grew solemn. "I always thought I'd be overjoyed at his death," Larke murmured, "but I just feel disturbed. How could a person let so much darkness into himself?"

Kempe walked into the woods, and returned shortly. "The one in there is unconscious," he told them.

"But he won't be a threat when he wakes, weakened and on his own."

They walked to where their horses waited patiently, along with the horses of the fallen riders. There they removed the saddles and bridles from the extra horses and let the animals loose to graze. The saddles and bridles they left on the ground.

"When that man wakes," Larke said, "he can call his horse, and have something to ride on."

Brandun turned toward the Temple of Wisdom. The glitter of sunlight on the jasper and crystal grew more dazzling, until the whole building dissolved into thousands of points of light which flickered and faded, and finally all Brandun could see was the green mountain slope, and shadows of drifting clouds. Looking up, Brandun gazed into the vastness of the sky, the blue that stretched far beyond his vision, and at the majesty of towering white clouds, so massive and yet so light.

"There's just so much — room," he exclaimed softly, struggling to explain his feeling. "So much room to grow, and — so much more to life than we usually see."

Quietly, thoughtfully, the companions prepared their horses for the homeward ride.

It took two days to travel out of the Jahaziel Mountains, two days of cheerful companionship with much to talk about. They had no trouble finding edible plants and roots and fresh mountain spring water, as if someone had carefully provided for them. The weather was kind, and the nights peaceful. They met no one, and so focused only on each other. Brandun pushed away any thoughts of approaching good-byes whenever they pricked at him.

The morning after their second night since leaving the Temple of Wisdom, the companions started up the last foothill leading away from the mountains. Brandun paused at the top, stopping his horse for just a moment to take a last close look at the Jahaziel range. The peaceful forested mountains stood quietly, regally, hiding their secrets. With a full heart, Brandun turned away and pointed his face toward home.

Chapter 24

The three slept on their cloaks that night, under a warm, clear sky. When the glow of dawn chased away the stars, Brandun awoke to find Larke tugging at his sleeve. Kempe was already sitting up.

"I've had a dream," she told them, looking shaken, "of someone at Thearl's manor. Whoever it was held a hand tightly over my mouth, so I could hardly breath. He was angry at us, and especially at me."

Brandun glanced at Kempe, then back at Larke. "With Thearl gone, who else at his manor could be dangerous to you?" he asked.

Larke bowed her head in thought. "His steward, I suppose, or any of his men who were loyal to him." Looking up, she added, "But I don't know how many of his men were loyal, and how many obeyed him out of fear. Thearl would threaten to harm innocent family members of the people he wanted to control."

"Do you want to come back to our castle with us?" Kempe inquired.

Larke shook her head fiercely. "I must see my family," she insisted. "I must see if my father's all right."

"Then we'll take you home," Kempe promised, "and we'll have to be ready for trouble."

Brandun gazed back toward the Jahaziel Mountains. Outside the mountains, he couldn't see the Light. Would it still help them?

It took almost three more days of travel to reach Thearl's manor, and without knowing what trouble awaited them, they couldn't plan how to deal with it.

Larke sped up when her village came into view. Brandun saw ahead the familiar wood and plaster houses with thatched roofs, the small hills dotted with sheep. They passed the men who cut hay in the fields, and the women who raked it into piles to be bundled. Many stopped to stare at the three riders who cantered toward the village.

When they entered the group of houses, a wheelwright skillfully forming pieces of curved wood into a wheel looked up from his work. "Why, its Marshal's daughter!" he exclaimed as they passed by. Heads turned to watch their arrival, and the street was quickly buzzing with excited chatter. Three young boys walking on wooden stilts in the road leaped off their toys and scrambled out of the horses' way.

"I'm going to tell Marshal!" one shouted, breaking into a run toward the stables. "Larke is back!"

"Mother! Father!" Larke called urgently as she halted in front of her home. She slid off her horse and bolted into the arms of a woman with straw-colored hair who ran out of the house. Brandun and Kempe stayed on their mounts, enjoying the happy scene, but alert to possible danger for Larke.

"Larke! My Larke!" the woman cried out, nearly crushing Larke in her arms. "Thearl went after you! We didn't know what would happen." She started to sob. Three boys ran out and pulled at their mother's arms, trying to get to their big sister. The two older sisters, one with a baby on her hip, soon arrived with their husbands from nearby cottages and threw their arms around the whole group. There was much crying and talking all at once, and the neighbors watched with tearful smiles.

"Please, you must let me through," a man's voice insisted loudly from behind the crowd.

Larke caught the sound and loosened herself from her family's hold. "Father?" she called.

The crowd parted to let Marshal through, and he locked his daughter tightly in his arms, moaning with relief.

"Father," Larke demanded, pushing back a bit. "Are you all right? Did Thearl punish you?"

"It's all in the past, my angel," he answered, taking her face in his hands. "I was given a hearty flogging, but Thearl values my services, and didn't damage me seriously." Larke burst into tears and threw herself against his chest again, where he rocked her gently from side to side.

"There, there now," he soothed. "I'm feeling nothing but joy right now."

Brandun felt the burning of tears behind his eyes, and he swallowed hard. Then three formidable figures caught his eye, pushing their way through the crowd.

They were richly dressed men from Thearl's manor, one apparently the steward, the one left in charge while Thearl was gone. One by one, the people in the crowd hushed at the sight of these men, until all was quiet, and the steward and his companions stood in front of Marshal and Larke. Marshal tightened his grip around his daughter protectively.

"Is this the runaway villein?" the steward questioned, his voice high and sharp. Marshal's brows lowered in anger, but he said nothing.

"Thearl is dead," Kempe announced bluntly. Many gasps went up from the crowd, and the tight face of the steward went pale as he turned toward Kempe, scowling.

"What proof do you have of this?" he demanded.

"I have no proof," Kempe responded.

"You'd best watch how you speak to the royal princes, Kempe and Brandun," Marshal remarked coldly.

The steward went still paler, and his bravado disappeared. "I beg your majesties' pardon," he stammered, greatly flustered, "but this is shocking news." The steward pondered the ramifications of Thearl's death for a moment, his mouth and nose contorting into amazing positions as he thought. "If this is true," he finally said, "since Thearl has no heir, ownership of Thearl's possessions would go to me. I must have time to consider the changes this will bring about. I beg your leave."

With that, the steward turned abruptly and scurried back into the manor, followed by the two other men.

As soon as they were gone, the villagers surrounding Larke and her family burst into excited questions about

Thearl's death. Larke answered as many as she could, and when she revealed that Brandun was now heir to the kingdom of Haefen, people stared at him in awe. Soon, though, Larke wished to go into her house and be alone with her family. The people outside continued to converse happily, greatly relieved that their tyrant lord would no longer trouble them.

"Will the steward be any better?" Brandun overheard one man ask.

"Oh, he won't be half so bad," answered another. "He was mostly just Thearl's frightened dog."

"A frightened dog can surely bite, though," added a woman. "He may carry on much the same."

Gradually, more and more people stopped to stare curiously at Brandun and Kempe atop their horses, the noble princes who had rescued Larke and conquered Thearl. When things had quieted to a murmur, Brandun cleared his throat and called out, "I don't think we'll be welcome guests at the manor. Can anyone find room for Prince Kempe and I to spend the night?"

"That I can!" shouted the wheelwright enthusiastically, but then he pulled off his hat and twisted it in his hands, embarrassed. "Of course," he apologized, "my place is nothing fancy. All I can offer are simple straw mattresses, and a share of my food. It may be too modest for your majesties."

Brandun grinned. "We've been sleeping on the ground for several weeks. Your offer sounds wonderful." The crowd laughed, and friendly chatter began anew. The wheelwright approached Brandun's horse.

"My house is the first you passed when you entered the village," he informed them, pointing. "I'll be getting the evening meal soon."

Brandun turned to Kempe. "There's something I'd like to do at the manor first," he confided softly. "I want to find that servant who helped us escape. He'll want to know what happened to us."

"I don't think we should risk going in," Kempe advised. "We don't know how many in there are loyal to Thearl, or what kind of people they are. Let's find a way to have the servant come outside."

Brandun turned back to the wheelwright. "There is something we must do first," he told him. "Then we'll happily join you for food."

"That'll be fine," the man responded cheerfully. "If you'll not be needing your horses, I can tether them behind my house." Kempe and Brandun dismounted and let the wheelwright lead the horses away while they headed toward the manor. They circled the stone building, approaching the door toward the back through which they had escaped many days before. Just then, a kitchen maid came out to empty her cooking water.

Impulsively, Brandun decided to ask her about the servant. "Hello," he called to her, and she turned to look at him. "I am Prince Brandun," he began.

"Yes," she replied, dropping a curtsey. "I remember when you stayed here, your majesty."

"We want to speak with a certain servant here," he continued. "He is a small, bald man, and he stutters quite badly."

The girl blinked rapidly, looking uncomfortable. "That servant — has died, sir," she said.

"What?" Brandun gasped. "How?"

The girl wrung her hands, and her lower lip trembled.

Kempe took her by the arm and looked into her eyes. "How?" he repeated.

"Oh, your majesties," she whispered, her voice squeaking, "he was executed for helping you to take that girl away. And I can't be seen talking to you." She shook her arm loose fearfully and ran back into the kitchen.

Brandun was stunned. His stomach felt as though someone had kicked it. He and Kempe stood motionless for several minutes, trying to absorb what she had said. Then rage started to build within Brandun, and he pounded his thighs with his fists. "No, no, no," he growled through his teeth. "The man helped us, and that snake Thearl had him killed!"

"I guess Thearl didn't value that servant's services as much as Marshal's," Kempe muttered. Grasping Brandun's shoulder, he spoke firmly. "Let's go back to the wheelwright's house."

Their steps were heavy as they walked. "Where was the Light when that servant needed help?" Brandun asked bitterly. "What kind of God would let a man be killed for aiding people to escape from harm?" He thought of the all powerful Light in the Jahaziel Mountains, guiding them and strengthening them against evil forces. But outside the Mountains, pain and cruelty and death went on.

Kempe offered no answer. The wheelwright was at his doorway when they arrived, beaming with hospitality. "A modest supper is ready for your majesties," he announced, leading them inside his home. Inside, Brandun saw that it was a strongly built, one room house, with two oilcloth windows to let in the light. Against one wall in tidy order leaned several wheels in various stages of completion. A saw, an awl, a hammer, and a plane for smoothing wood lay next to the wheels, as well as a pile of wooden pegs.

"You do fine work," Kempe commented, inspecting the wheels.

"Thearl kept me busy," the man responded, "though he always found some complaint about my work." He sat on a bench at a smooth wooden table and gestured for them to join him. Brandun sullenly sat next to him, and Kempe followed.

"As sure as the stars above, something's troubling you," the wheelwright observed, eyeing Brandun's face.

Kempe explained what they had learned about the stuttering servant. The wheelwright heaved a sigh and shook his head.

"That was terrible news," he remembered. "Thearl was always cruel, doing public floggings and such, but we didn't expect him to go so far. He claimed he had the right, because he owns us all, and he could enforce his rules as he wished."

Kempe continued to converse with the wheelwright, but Brandun found it hard to pay attention. His anger and confusion exhausted him, and he felt that all was hopeless. He couldn't stop harm from coming to good people. There was too much to stop.

After supper, Brandun sank onto a straw mattress, his body heavy and his mind still clouded. *Where is the Light?* he asked again in his mind. *Where are You in this world full of troubles below the Mountains?* Crickets chirped in steady rhythm, finally lulling him to sleep.

Chapter 25

When Brandun woke, it was still dark, but a faint tone of gray in the east showed him that dawn was near. He had woken suddenly from a dream that confused him. Kempe and the wheelwright still slept contentedly, so he rose and crept outside. Sparke greeted him with a soft whinny and nibbled at his shoulder affectionately. Brandun rummaged through his saddle bag which lay on the ground, wishing for a fresh change of clothing. All he found was the clothing Lufu had given him. His other royal traveling clothes had been burned back at Tamtun after he had helped battle the plague of fever.

After changing quickly into the common clothing, he picked up a large bucket that sat next to the house and headed for the town well. Pulling the dripping bucket up, he washed his hands and face and rinsed his mouth, all the while pondering the dream that had awakened him. He thrust his royal tunic into the bucket, sloshing it around to rinse it, then spread it out on the grass to dry. When he had finished washing his cloak and leggings, he felt a sudden urge to see Larke. She, he thought, could help him with his dream.

The golden glow of morning had taken over most of

the sky by the time he reached Larke's house. He rapped at the door, but when it opened, the hazel eyes that looked at him were not Larke's.

"Prince Brandun!" Larke's mother exclaimed. She threw the door open and drew him in. "Larke has gone out with her sisters to wash," she explained. "She was mighty filthy after that journey." Putting a hand on Brandun's back, she guided him to sit down on a bench, then sat beside him and impulsively took his hand. "I am Nara. You and Prince Kempe have been good to my daughter," she said warmly. "God bless you both."

"It was nice to have her with us," Brandun responded awkwardly. Then he realized that this woman could help him with his dream, perhaps better than Larke. He cleared his throat. "Larke tells me that you know much about dreams."

Nara released his hand. "Yes," she confirmed. "The study of dreams has been passed down in my family from mother to daughter." She paused a moment, then asked, "You have had a dream?"

Brandun nodded. "This morning."

"Tell me," she encouraged him softly.

Brandun shifted on his bench, then began. "In the dream, a messenger came with a gift for me. It was a bowl, beautifully painted. As he handed me the bowl, he said, 'In these', and then was gone. I looked into the bowl, and suddenly I was *in* the bowl, and so were some other people."

"What people?" Nara questioned.

"Kempe was there," said Brandun, "and Larke. Also

Lufu, a woman I met in Tamtun, and the bald-headed servant who was killed, and your husband, and Ladroc, our steward back at the castle, and Queen Aeldra, and even the wheelwright who took us in last night. There seemed to be many other people there, too, but I couldn't tell who they were."

"I see," said Nara. "And how did you feel about these people in the bowl with you?"

"I felt how wonderful they all were," said Brandun, "and what goodness they have brought to my life."

"And the messenger who brought the bowl?"

Brandun thought for a moment. "He was very good and very kind," he remembered. "The goodness flowed out of him, like it had from two people we met in the Jahaziel Mountains."

"And the bowl was a gift?"

"Yes."

"And so, it seems, were the things in the bowl," Nara murmured, rubbing her chin. "Now, the first thing the messenger said was 'In these'?"

Brandun nodded.

"It sounds like an answer to a question," Nara noted. "Have you asked an important question recently, either out loud or in your own head?"

Brandun thought a moment, and quickly remembered his burning question the night before as he was lying in bed. *Where is the Light? Where are You?* It felt so personal he was hesitant to tell Nara, but realized he must if he wanted her help. "I was asking God something," he said slowly. "I asked where He was."

194

"And the answer," Nara continued for him, "is '*in these.*'"

Brandun looked at her. "In the people in the bowl?" he asked.

"In their *goodness,*" Nara clarified. "That's what you noticed about them in the dream, isn't it?"

"So," Brandun responded hesitantly, "that would mean God is in the goodness of all those people I know, and many other people that I don't know." He felt a tingle of hope, because it made sense.

"Notice also," Nara pointed out, "that you yourself were in the bowl, meaning God is also present in your own good virtues. So where is God? In the things that you love in others, and feel good about in yourself — bravery, loyalty, friendship, compassion, kindness, and much more. These things are God's gifts, and God's presence." Nara smiled. "It is a beautiful message, Brandun."

"The Light *is* here," said Brandun softly. "I just have to look for it differently."

At that moment, Larke entered the house with her sisters. Her hair draped over her shoulders, sleek and wet. She wore a simple, loose-fitting dress of faded blue, and the familiar dimples appeared in her cheeks when she saw Brandun.

"Your friend has come to visit," Nara declared cheerfully. Brandun realized he was staring at Larke — he had never seen her looking so feminine — and he hurriedly dropped his eyes. "Will you join us for our morning meal?" Nara offered. Brandun's stomach rumbled in answer, and everyone laughed.

In the late afternoon, Brandun sat with Kempe in the shadow cast by the wheelwright's house. Both were itchy with idleness, wondering whether the steward would still want to punish Larke as a runaway, and what kind of protection she would need. The breeze blew lazily, and a pleasant hum drifted from the beehive the wheelwright kept at the edge of his property as a source of honey. They talked of home and what they might find there, and then Brandun told Kempe about his dream, and the meaning Nara had helped him gather from it.

"It is a comforting thought," Kempe agreed, "that the Light is here in people's goodness. I still wonder, though, why evil is allowed to exist, and people allowed to harm each other."

"I'm not sure," said Brandun. "But Eadric told me in a dream that after death, real life begins. And there, the evil can't harm the good any more." Then he realized something. "The servant who helped us is there now, where Eadric is." He and Kempe were quiet a moment, considering that thought.

"And perhaps he doesn't stutter any more," Kempe added.

The sun was dropping low in the sky when a message came. "One of Thearl's men came back from the Jahaziel Mountains, very ill," said a breathless boy. "He said for certain Thearl is dead!"

"That would be the one we left in the woods, up where we found the Temple of Wisdom," said Brandun.

"We'd best go to the manor," Kempe advised.

Brandun snatched his dried royal traveling clothes

from off the grass and bolted into the wheelwright's house. There he changed, and he and Kempe put on their belts and swords. Carefully, Brandun tucked the golden scepter in his belt as well, and then he and Kempe headed for the manor.

As they approached the stone building, a servant met them. "Our former steward," he reported, "who, because of Lord Thearl's death, is now our new Lord Holcumb, is not ready to see you. He begs your majesties' pardons, but with the confirmation of Lord Thearl's death, Lord Holcumb has much business to sort out." With that, the servant turned and trotted back into the manor.

Brandun looked at Kempe and shrugged. "Let's go over to Larke's cottage."

They found Nara cleaning up from the evening meal while Marshal sat patting his stomach contentedly. The younger boys were playing marbles on the floor.

"Where is Larke?" Brandun asked, immediately noticing her absence in the one room home.

Marshal turned toward them and smiled in welcome. "She had been helping me tend to the horses this afternoon," he told them. "She ran back just now to put a dressing on an ulcer we found on one horse's leg."

"She must not be alone," Brandun warned. "She may be in danger."

Kempe touched him on the arm. "Let's go," he urged.

"But Lord Thearl is dead," Marshal called after them in confusion as they ran out toward the stable.

"She must not have told her family about that last dream," Kempe panted as they ran.

197

"What was she thinking, to go out alone?" Brandun wondered anxiously.

They reached the stables and called out her name, but received no answer. With panic mounting in his chest, Brandun ran around the outside of the stable while Kempe searched more thoroughly inside. Brandun heard a faint thump at the back of the structure, and ran faster, pulling his sword out as he went. In his mind, he saw a large hand clapped over Larke's mouth, as she had dreamed.

Once behind the stable, he slowed his pace to search the brush and small trees. With his heart pounding and his sword ready, he pushed aside the bushes one by one.

Then suddenly, there she was. Brandun cried out, startled, and ripped the branch he had pushed aside right off the bush. Larke's eyes were wide and pleading, and over her mouth was a large, hairy hand. Behind her, holding her tightly against him, glowered the same angry man who had threatened to run a sword through Kempe; the same man whom Larke had knocked down with a rock. Fitch! His other hand held a dagger at her stomach.

"Kempe!" Brandun shouted, keeping his eyes on Fitch and his sword in front of him. Kempe arrived quickly and stood behind Brandun's shoulder.

"Surprised to see me alive?" Fitch snarled. "This murderous wench nearly killed me."

"Only to save my life," Kempe shot back.

"You all left me for dead, even Thearl," Fitch growled. "There I awoke, my own blood crusted on me, and a headache like I've never felt before. Had to drag

198

myself home alone. And all because of this foolish, run-away girl. I want justice!"

Brandun heard the sounds of running, and anxious voices. Marshal, Nara, and their children rounded the corner of the barn. When she caught sight of Larke, Nara covered her mouth to stifle a cry, and Kempe signaled them to be still. Soon more villeins arrived, and quietly formed a half circle around the scene.

Fitch grew more nervous. "You all stay back," he ordered, tightening his hold on Larke. She moaned and pulled at his hand that blocked her breath.

Fear gripped Brandun so hard it hurt. He looked at Fitch's dagger against Larke's stomach, and knew that a sword would not get him out of this one. Numbly, he put it back into its sheath. What could he do? What if he couldn't save her?

I must keep my head, he told himself. *It seems that I can't save her, but...but the Light can give me the power.* Brandun let his shoulders relax ever so slightly at the thought. Yes. He must keep dark fear and anger from blocking it.

Where was the Light right now? Brandun took a deep breath, keeping his eyes fixed on Fitch, and tried to feel it. There! He felt Kempe's strong, comforting presence right behind his shoulder. Beyond that were the silent, good villeins, standing ready to help.

And within himself? Brandun fought to silence the futile, frightened thoughts that raced through his mind, and suddenly a quiet idea entered, as if from the back of his head.

"Someone fetch Lord Holcumb," he directed firmly, "and tell him to bring armed guards. Tell him there's trouble." One of Larke's brothers sprinted off, and in the fading light, Fitch and Brandun continued to glare at each other.

Lord Holcumb and three guards arrived with a clatter of swords. "This wench is a runaway," Fitch shouted angrily, "and she tried to murder me! I want to see her punished!"

"Fitch!" Lord Holcumb scolded pompously, trying on his new authority. "The girl is my villein. You will give her to me to be dealt with."

"Only if you guarantee her punishment," Fitch insisted through gritted teeth. "Give me my revenge, and Thearl's!"

"I must point out, Lord Holcumb," Brandun interrupted, "that Fitch tried to murder Prince Kempe, and Larke took action against Fitch only to rescue him. Violence against a member of the royal family is a serious crime."

"Oh!" exclaimed Holcumb in a shocked voice. "I always knew that Fitch was trouble. Fitch," he commanded, wagging a finger toward the man, "release the girl! She will receive her punishment, and you will receive yours."

Like a cornered animal, Fitch tightened his grip again, and Larke moaned. Brandun's hand shot out toward him.

"Stop, Fitch!" he shouted. "If you harm her, your punishment will be much more grievous."

"She's only a villein," Fitch growled back. "It is no serious crime to... ."

A new idea shot into Brandun's mind. "She's no longer only a villein," he declared. Pulling the golden scepter from his belt, he held it up, and it caught the last rays of the setting sun. "This scepter," he went on, "is a sign from the Temple of Wisdom in the Jahaziel Mountains that I am the chosen heir to the throne of Haefen. And I, the next king, have chosen Larke for my future wife."

Soft exclamations went up from the people behind him, and Larke's hazel eyes widened. "But — your majesty," Holcumb protested. "She's a lowly commoner! And she's *my* lowly commoner!"

"As king, I am entitled to a share of your goods each year," Brandun told the flustered lord. "I have chosen my goods." Turning back toward Fitch, he looked the desperate man right in the eye and threatened, "There's no escape, Fitch. The punishment for harming the next queen of Haefen is *very* grievous. Let her go."

All were silent. With a signal from Kempe, Holcumb's guards moved slowly forward. Fitch looked hopelessly from Brandun, to the guards, and then back to Brandun. Finally, with an angry grunt, he shoved Larke forward so that she sprawled onto the grass. Before Brandun could move, Nara rushed over and clasped her daughter against her.

"Curse you all," Fitch spat out bitterly, "and curse Lord Thearl. My whole life has been cursed!"

Holcumb's guards caught his arms and led him away.

Nara and Marshal whisked Larke back toward their house, but not without earnest looks of gratitude as they passed Brandun.

"Haefen will be blessed to have such a king," said Marshal, his voice deep with emotion. Larke's look was one of stunned silence. She opened her mouth, but nothing came out. Nara urged her forward, murmuring soothing words.

Other people passed, speaking soft words of gratitude and respect, but Brandun couldn't make them out. He realized that he was still holding the scepter aloft, and that he was shivering. Night was falling, and a chill breeze blew from behind him.

Kempe's hand came to rest on his shoulder, firm and comforting. "You did that one yourself," he said.

"With the help of God," Brandun whispered.

In the morning, Brandun quickly washed and ate at the wheelwright's house before heading to Larke's home.

"I'll saddle both horses and pack provisions," Kempe called after him, "but we must leave soon."

Brandun nodded gratefully. "Thank you. I won't be long."

Soon he arrived at Marshal's home, where Marshal stood in the doorway and greeted him with a smile. "Come in," he welcomed, leading Brandun through the door. The chattering of the family stopped when he entered. Larke, at the small trestle table with her brothers and sisters, blushed when she saw him and looked down at her breakfast bread. Brandun swallowed hard. Could they ever speak normally to each other again, now that he had made that declaration the night before?

"Prince Brandun," Nara greeted warmly. "Will you eat with us?"

Brandun cleared his throat. "I have eaten, thank you. I — Kempe and I must leave today. We have things to take care of back at home. But before I go, I want all of you to know that — that I won't be like Thearl and force Larke into marriage." He looked down, avoiding Larke's face. "I said that to rescue her, and I will hold to it if she wishes, when I am old enough. But Larke is free to decide for herself, and there is plenty of time."

There was an awkward moment of silence. Larke's brothers and sisters stared at her curiously, wondering what she would say to this. But Larke said nothing.

Marshal clapped Brandun about the shoulders. "You honor my daughter and my family greatly, by asking for her hand," he assured Brandun. "But you are right, there is time to think, so we will let Larke do so. You need a few years on you yet, until you're ready to become a husband," he teased. Brandun reached up self-consciously to smooth his brown curls.

"Well, I must go. Kempe is waiting," he said. "You are all good people, and I wish you well." The family members bade him farewell, but Larke still looked down at her bread.

"Well," said Brandun again. "Good-bye." He turned to leave the cottage.

"Brandun," Larke said quickly.

He turned back.

"I'll walk with you and Kempe to the edge of the village." She rose to follow him, as Nara pushed half a loaf of bread and some cheese into her hands.

"Give this to the princes," she told her. "I wish it was more," she apologized to Brandun, "but with a large family, there's not much to spare."

Brandun thanked her, then left with Larke. She looked down at her hands as they walked, and spoke.

"This feels different," she commented. "I hadn't thought before about marrying a good friend."

"I want us to stay friends," he entreated. "You don't have to... ."

"I know," Larke responded quietly. "And you don't have to, either, because I know you were trying to rescue me. We both have time to think. And *I* think," she added, finally looking up at him, "that it may turn out to be a nice idea."

Back at the wheelwright's house, Kempe had the horses ready. Brandun was touched to find many people of the village gathered to see them off.

"They brought generous gifts of food," Kempe told him, patting their bulging saddle bags.

"A first token of homage to our next king, and to the captain of his armed forces," declared the wheelwright. The princes thanked the people for the food, and the wheelwright for his hospitality.

"It was an honor," he replied with a grin.

With waves and farewells, Brandun and Kempe parted from the people and walked, leading their horses, beside Larke. She was dressed again in boy's clothing,

"I'll be riding today with my father," she explained, her hair neatly braided behind her. Brandun stole glances at her face, trying to memorize the hazel eyes, the sprinkling of freckles, the soft dimples in each cheek, and the loose wisps of straw-colored hair that blew in the breeze. His chest ached as they drew near the road.

They halted at the road, and were silent a moment. "It won't be easy to get used to life without you again," Larke said, finally. Kempe took her hand and kissed it.

"I was foolishly unsure about taking you along at first," he told her. "I am now glad you were with us. You taught us things, and brought a brightness we wouldn't have had on our own."

Larke smiled, then put her arms around him in a farewell hug.

How does Kempe think of such wonderful things to say? Brandun wondered, frantically trying to decide whether he, too, should kiss her hand. From Kempe, these things came more naturally. But before he could act, Larke turned to him and wrapped her arms around his neck, holding him tightly against her. Gratefully, he hugged her and tried to speak.

"I..." he began, but his throat tightened, and he had to swallow.

"I'll miss you too, Brandun," she said softly. She released him — had she perhaps held him a little longer than Kempe? — and Brandun flushed hotly as he felt her lips brush against his cheek. Larke smiled at him, though her eyes were wet.

"I hope I'll see you again soon — both of you," she said.

"Will you come to the ceremony declaring I'm heir to the throne?" he asked.

"I want to," she answered. "Send us word."

The princes mounted, then started their horses along the road.

"Good-bye," Brandun called, and Larke waved in response. He looked back at her a while, then realized Kempe's eyes were on him.

"A fine girl, isn't she, little cousin?" he teased with a twinkle in his eye.

Brandun's cheeks grew warm, and he grinned sheepishly. Then, tapping Sparke's gray sides with his heels, he took off at a trot, leaving Kempe to chuckle behind him.

Chapter 26

It took six days of riding to get to the castle. Brandun and Kempe talked of Lord Bardaric, wondering about the state of affairs back home. Brandun wished they could stop in the town of Tamtun, to see how Lufu and the rest of the townspeople were doing, but he and Kempe agreed that they must waste no time. Their worry increased with each passing day.

But when the castle came into view, in the late afternoon of the sixth day, Brandun felt a surge of excitement. The familiar turrets stirred his memories of home, and he thought he would burst with longing. Kempe must have experienced something similar, because he urged his horse into a canter at the same moment Brandun did, and they both laughed with relief and joy.

They rode to the castle gate and yelled to the gate-keepers, who happily lowered the drawbridge across the moat and lifted the iron portcullis, shouting a greeting as the princes passed. Clattering into the stables, Brandun and Kempe slid off their mounts and pounded the surprised stablehands on the back in greeting, then asked them to walk and put away the horses. In the courtyard, people tending livestock stopped their activities to call a cheerful welcome. A lad pushing a wheelbarrow full of hay set it down to wave, and another, sharpening his knife at a spinning wheel of stone abandoned the task to go spread the news. A girl drawing a bucket from the well dropped it back down in surprise, and faces appeared at windows and doors in the servants' cottages. Brandun and Kempe returned the greetings, uplifted by all the happy chatter, and strode toward the large castle keep, where Aeldra and Defena would be waiting.

They passed a girl working at a wooden butter churn. She turned to dip a cheerful curtsy, and in doing so, knocked over the churn. It hit the ground with a thud, loosening the lid, and the thick cream oozed onto the ground.

"Oh!" the girl cried out, frantically grabbing at the churn to set it upright again. But it was too late. Almost all the cream lay in a puddle at her feet. "Oh, oh, oh," she whimpered, clapping her hands to her cheeks.

"It's all right," Brandun assured her. "There'll be more cream tomorrow, and there must be butter in the pantry somewhere."

"You don't understand," the girl told him, close to tears. "Lord Bardaric insisted on fresh butter for today's meal. He'll be so angry!"

Brandun and Kempe looked at each other. "Does Lord Bardaric give orders to the queen's servants?" Kempe asked.

"Oh, yes," the girl replied, sniffing. "To all of us. He says he must take care of things for Queen Aeldra."

Their homecoming joy now subdued, Brandun and

Kempe left the girl and continued on toward the keep. Bursting into the great hall, Brandun called out urgently, "Aeldra! Aeldra, it's Brandun and Kempe!" Startled servants looked their way with frightened faces, and one young man hurriedly approached them.

"Your majesties," he said in a hushed, anxious voice, bowing low. "We are overjoyed to see you safely home, but it is at this time each day that we are ordered by Lord Bardaric to be extremely quiet and not, under any circumstances, disturb queen Aeldra's rest period. Anyone who does will be severely punished."

Brandun now noticed around the room armed guards he did not recognize. Apparently Bardaric had moved in some of his own people to enforce his rules.

"Queen Aeldra's rest period?" Brandun repeated.

"Yes," confirmed the servant in a whisper, glancing nervously at a guard that strolled closer. "Lord Bardaric has been taking good care of Queen Aeldra since her husband's death. He attends to her every need, shows her every kindness, and treats roughly anyone who may interfere with the recovery of her health and good spirits. That is why he insists so strongly on her private rest period, which he supervises himself. He says she must rest each day to gain back her strength."

Brandun looked over at Kempe, who's furrowed brow revealed his concern. Just then a man and a woman entered the hall from the other side and hurried toward the princes as quickly as they could without making excessive noise. Brandun's heart leaped when he made out the face of Ladroc, Eadric's own dear steward. The woman was Defena, and she had eyes only for Kempe. Making straight for her son, she tried to control her expression, but Brandun could see the longing. When she reached him, her face tightened with emotion. She buried her face in Kempe's shoulder, holding him silently as he wrapped her in his arms.

"Mother," he said gently, stroking her long braided hair, as richly auburn as his own.

Ladroc reached Brandun and clasped him against his chest. "Thank God you are home," he sighed anxiously. He glanced toward Kempe and Defena. "We'll leave those two to talk," he decided. "Come with me to your bedchamber." Quickly, he released Brandun and turned toward the spiral stone staircase that led upwards. Brandun followed, swiftly and quietly, aware of suspicious stares from Lord Bardaric's guards.

Up in Brandun's chamber, Ladroc closed the door and took Brandun by the shoulders. "Things are bad," he said gravely. "I don't know what that snake is doing to the queen. In front of everyone, he treats her with tender kindness, protecting her from everything. But in spite of his care, the queen looks weaker and weaker. She has a lost expression in her eyes, and depends upon him more and more to make decisions. Bardaric's guards obey their conniving master. Eadric's guards still obey only the queen. She never speaks ill of the snake, so I am powerless to do anything! Brandun," he moaned, letting go of the boy and pacing the floor. "I'm afraid for her, and for Haefen."

"Lord Bardaric stays with her during this rest period?" Brandun asked.

Ladroc turned toward him sharply. "Yes!" he answered. "He, and no one else. I worry terribly about what goes on in her chamber during this time, but the room is always guarded, and all are warned to stay away."

"Surely, they'll let *me* in," Brandun asserted, moving toward his door determinedly. "I'm the prince, just back from a journey. Aeldra will want to see me right away!"

"I do not know, Brandun," Ladroc began doubtfully, but Brandun was already in the hall. He marched straight for Aeldra's chamber door, and halted in front of two muscular guards.

"I'm Prince Brandun, back from a journey to the Jahaziel Mountains. Queen Aeldra will certainly want to see me immediately, so please announce that I'm here."

The guards looked at each other, then one spoke. "Your majesty, forgive me, but we must wait until after the queen's rest period, by orders of Lord Bardaric and the Queen herself."

Brandun was taken aback. "The Queen's orders?"

"Yes. The Queen is not in good health and badly needs her rest. She insists on it."

"But surely she'll see me," Brandun repeated lamely.

"Please don't ask me to disobey the queen, your majesty," the guard requested firmly.

Brandun stood for a moment, perplexed, then headed back to his own bedchamber and closed the door.

"So you see," said Ladroc.

"I see," Brandun muttered.

Ladroc shook his head hopelessly. "I've tried divert-ing the guards, but they will not be diverted."

"Hah!" said Brandun, breaking into a sudden grin. "Find me a rope, Ladroc, and I'll climb down from the roof into the west window."

Ladroc blinked. "Well, I never thought of that," he admitted. "Of course, even if I had, I wouldn't have had the agility..."

"Go!" Brandun whispered impatiently, pushing him toward the door. Ladroc left, and Brandun paced about the room until the steward reappeared with a rope con-cealed beneath his robe.

Together they went quietly to the spiral stairway and ascended to the roof. Scattered gray clouds spotted the sky, and a greater mass of them was collecting on the horizon. The wind was picking up.

"Good," said Brandun, hurriedly pulling the rope from beneath Ladroc's robe. "The wind may help hide any noises I make." He shed his sword and laid it on the ground. It would be too noisy and cumbersome to take on his climb. Pulling the scepter from his belt, he stud-ied it a moment. *It is bonded to your spirit,* the golden man had said. *It is a symbol of the king you will be, and of your specific strengths.* It was the symbol of his new authority, and Brandun knew he must have it with him when he confronted Bardaric. Being smaller than the sword, the scepter slid easily down the back of his tunic, where his belt held it in place.

Brandun walked to the edge where he thought the west window would be and leaned over the side. The height from four stories up made him dizzy, and he couldn't see the window in the flat wall below him.

"I can't see the window," he told Ladroc. "I'll have to guess where it is, and hope I come down near enough to reach it."

Together they decided the window was about four paces from the corner of the keep. After measuring that distance, Ladroc wrapped the rope twice around a section of stone that jutted up from the wall. "If I wrap it any more, it might not hang down far enough," he pointed out. "I'll knot it, but I'll still hold fast to the end while you're climbing."

"Well," said Brandun, when all was ready, looking hesitantly over the edge.

"It's best to go quickly, before thinking about it too much," advised Ladroc, gripping the end of the rope securely. "Kick off your shoes."

After doing so, Brandun swung one leg over the wall and lay on his stomach. Then he swung the other leg over. Trembling a bit, he seized the rope, and with a deep breath lowered his body over the edge. The rope was harsh against his hands, and the stone wall rough on his feet. He inched his way down, seeking out the top edges of stones with his bare toes. Once he hit his knee painfully, and had to clench his teeth to keep from crying out. The west wall faced away from the main courtyard, so there was no one below to glance upward and spot him.

Soon he saw the top of the window, just off to his right, and stretched his leg toward it. For an instant, he saw the distant ground below him and was seized with fear. He stifled a gasp, closed his eyes, and fought to keep his hands from losing their grip. *I must pretend the ground is just below my feet,* he thought. He spent a moment picturing the ground close below him, while the wind pushed him from behind. Resolving not to look down, he opened his eyes.

Again, Brandun reached his right leg toward the window and hooked his foot into it. He inched his way down a little more, then pulled his body over with his leg. Panting, he shot a hand out and gripped the stone edge of the window. The rope swung precariously as his left hand strained to keep hold of it. Painful shots of panic raced from his chest and stomach down his limbs. For a moment he thought he would fall backward, and wanted to scream. But with a mighty push, he scraped his right leg further into the window, hooked his knee over the sill, and slid his arm into the room. He pulled until finally he was straddling the solid stone sill. Releasing the rope, Brandun hugged the thick stone wall in front of him, eyes closed, waiting for his pounding heart to calm.

Brandun was afraid to look into the room. Anxiously, he imagined Lord Bardaric's angry face glaring at him. He detected a hushed sound, barely audible over the wind. Brandun opened his eyes.

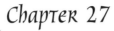

Chapter 27

The first thing Brandun saw was the great canopy bed, its curtains mostly drawn. But on one side, a man sat on a stool by the bed, leaning in through a gap in the curtains. Quietly, Brandun climbed out of the window and walked forward, his bare feet silent on the floor. As he made his way, he reached back and fumbled inside his shirt until he caught hold of the scepter and pulled it out.

Beside the bed, across from the man on the stool, Brandun stopped. He was hidden from those inside the curtained walls, and he turned his ear toward the cloth. The hushed sound was indeed Lord Bardaric, talking in steady, low tones. Unable to make out Bardaric's words, Brandun crept silently to a corner of the bed where he cautiously put his eye to a crack between the curtains.

Through the slit, he could see Queen Aeldra lying on the bed. Her eyes were half closed, her mouth slightly opened. She seemed to be in a daze. Right beside her, Bardaric whispered into her ear, talking on and on in steady, monotone rhythm.

With sudden anger, Brandun tore the curtain aside and shouted, "What are you doing?"

Aeldra cried out in shock and lay blinking at him, like someone who had just been woken from sleep. Lord Bardaric bolted up off his stool, knocking it to the ground. The bed curtain hindered his effort to stand, and he pushed it aside with great exasperation. When he looked back at Brandun, his eyebrows were lowered in fury.

"What is the meaning of this!" he demanded.

"What are you doing to her?" Brandun repeated angrily.

Aeldra's eyes began to focus, and a smile of recognition came to her face. "Brandun," she cried softly, tears appearing at the corners of her eyes. She reached her arms out eagerly. Brandun leaned over the bed toward her and reached one hand out to clasp the queen's.

"What is happening, Aeldra?" he pleaded. "Tell me."

The queen furrowed her brow, looking suddenly confused. "Why — I'm resting, Brandun," she explained hesitantly.

"Yes," Bardaric broke in, his voice silken smooth. Brandun looked up to see that same, condescending smile he remembered from this handsome lord. The man had collected himself, and stood looking stately and calm in a green satin robe, his honey-colored hair and beard neatly combed. "Forgive me, young prince," he went on, "but you startled me greatly. Weren't you told the rules about the queen's rest period? How did you get in?"

"I came through the window," Brandun informed him, "to find out what you were doing to Aeldra! Why does she need you speaking into her ear to help her rest?"

Without warning, Bardaric swiftly leaned over and snatched Brandun's hand, bending his fingers backward. Gasping in pain, Brandun dropped the scepter which he had been holding low at his side, out of sight, and it fell to the floor with a soft clunk. He clawed at Bardaric's hand with his loose one, but the lord's grip was powerful.

"Bardaric!" the queen objected. "What are you doing?"

"Come over here to me," Bardaric insisted through clenched teeth. He bent Brandun's fingers harder, and the prince yelped, thinking they would break. Quickly, Brandun scrambled across the bed on his knees and free hand. Pushing Aeldra forcefully over in the bed, Bardaric pulled the prince right across her. The grim lord then released Brandun's aching hand and pushed him down into the vacant space beside Aeldra, holding him fast by the shoulders.

"Bardaric...," the queen began again, her voice full of concern.

"Aeldra, look at me," Bardaric ordered as Brandun struggled beneath his grip. She looked into his eyes. "He is full of irrational anger," Bardaric reasoned firmly, as if talking to a child. "I must calm him down. You see how it is, don't you?" Aeldra's lips parted, as if she would speak. But under Bardaric's fixed gaze her face fell into confusion, and she looked suddenly tired. The queen closed her mouth and said no more.

The nobleman leaned close to Brandun and spoke.

"Let me go!" said Lord Bardaric, softly, but with urgency.

Brandun hesitated, confused. Bardaric was the one

217

holding him! Why did he ask to be let go? He struggled some more.

"Let me go," said Lord Bardaric again, louder. "Let me go!"

"Yes, let me go!" shouted Brandun.

"You're despicable," said Bardaric.

"Yes, you're despicable!" yelled Brandun. "You're a conniving..."

"...snake," Lord Bardaric finished.

"Yes — snake," stammered Brandun. "You're trying to..."

"...control Aeldra and the castle," Bardaric finished again.

"I don't..."

"...know what you are doing. What are you doing?" It was Lord Bardaric who spoke the words, but he was speaking Brandun's thoughts. How did he know Brandun's thoughts? Brandun looked Bardaric right in the eyes, and then could not look away. His body went limp. Bardaric's blue-gray eyes stared intently into his own. The stare seemed to bore into his skull, and hold him fast.

"Brandun," the nobleman whispered. "Listen to me."

"No," Brandun protested feebly, but Bardaric went on.

"Listen to me," he whispered again. "Listen only to me. You are young. You are tired from your journey. You need help and guidance."

Brandun drew in a breath to say something, but Bardaric breathed in at the very same time and spoke before Brandun could.

"You are young," he repeated. "You are tired. You need help and guidance."

Every time Brandun drew in a breath, Bardaric imitated his breathing and spoke before he could. Soon they were breathing in unison, and Brandun stopped trying to talk. Every time Bardaric spoke, Brandun exhaled slowly until the older man inhaled again, and Brandun inhaled as well. He was drifting — drifting on the whispered words, repeated over and over, and he felt that Bardaric was now breathing for him. It was soothing, relaxing — he didn't have to speak; he didn't have to breathe on his own; he didn't have to think....

"You need me," the whispering went on, and Brandun's eyes fell half closed. "I am strong and capable. I will care for things. I care tenderly for Aeldra. I will care for you. You are young. It is hard to make decisions. I will help you...."

All was quiet except for Bardaric's voice that continued on and on, and the rushing of the wind in the background, which blended soothingly with the voice. The black circles at the center of Bardaric's staring eyes seemed to grow larger, and Brandun felt that perhaps he could slip into them and go to sleep, relieved of all worries.

But then came a rumble of thunder. It rolled across the sky above the castle, breaking the stream of Bardaric's words. Brandun's mind flickered, pulling just a little away from the whispering.

Another clap of thunder, this one more piercing, split the quiet air, and this one seemed to Brandun to be a call. It was like a mighty voice, commanding Brandun to listen, and he shifted his eyes away from Bardaric's. As his eyes struggled to focus, he thought he saw a cloud of darkness around the nobleman's head.

Push away the darkness, said a thought. Realization seeped into his mind. Bardaric was trying to control his thinking. Slowly, his own thoughts began to stir again, and with a mighty effort, he struggled to breathe out when Bardaric was breathing in — and succeeded! Brandun's mind broke free. A memory rushed in, of tales Ladroc had told him as a boy, of long ago sorcerers who sought to control men's minds.

"Sorcery," he gasped, and suddenly Bardaric slapped his face.

"Bardaric!" exclaimed Aeldra in horror.

"He's being insolent," Bardaric reasoned, struggling to keep his voice calm. "I was trying to help him."

"He's trying to control us," Brandun contradicted, kicking and flailing his arms. Bardaric raised his arm to strike again, but Aeldra sat up suddenly and grabbed the arm. Brandun rolled off the bed, landing at Bardaric's feet, then scrambled away on all fours.

"Bardaric! Don't hurt him!" Aeldra entreated tearfully.

Bardaric glared at the prince, but turned to stroke Aeldra's cheek soothingly. "Calm down, my dear, you need to rest. Don't boys need to be disciplined some-times?"

Brandun stood and then ran around the bed, where he picked up the golden scepter. Dashing back, he thrust it out in front of him, displaying it to Bardaric and Aeldra, shaking from the effort of breaking free, and with anger.

"Look here, Lord Bardaric!" he ordered. "*I* am to be the next king! Powers higher than you or I have decided it!"

"Oh, Brandun," marveled Aeldra, gazing at the glistening golden horse. "You found the Temple of Wisdom! Your scepter is as beautiful as Eadric's was."

Bardaric's eyebrows lowered for a split second, but then his face relaxed and he laughed.

"Aeldra," he said in a silky voice, taking her hand, "surely a woman as intelligent as you does not make decisions based on a shiny piece of metal? I understand your fondness for this boy, but who has been helping you rule through all these difficult days? Your nephew has no experience in a position of authority. You and I, my dear, can make this kingdom great."

When Aeldra did not reply, only stared at his hand holding hers, he grew impatient. "Has all my help meant nothing? You'll honor only the rights of someone holding a golden fairy wand? Well, I can hold this wand as well as he." Releasing her hand, Lord Bardaric lunged forward, grasped the scepter and pulled. Brandun tried to hold on, but Bardaric was stronger, and the golden object was wrenched from his hand.

Lord Bardaric lifted the scepter high above his head. Brandun crouched slightly, ready to leap up and try to grab it back, but stopped short. In Bardaric's clenched fist, the scepter turned dark as soot. Aeldra gasped and put a hand to her mouth.

His eyes wide with alarm, Bardaric circled his other hand around the blackened scepter, muttering strange words. Suddenly, the scepter burst into flame. Bardaric cried out and dropped it, and it clattered onto the floor. There the scepter lay, burning with angry red fire. A pool of blood seeped out from it, staining the floor.

Brandun felt power flooding the room, the power of truth he had felt in the Jahaziel Mountains. He closed his eyes and opened his mind to it, and then he understood the strange sight.

Flinging his eyes open, he pointed a finger at Bardaric, and spoke.

"The scepter symbolizes the power of ruling," he shouted, "and the horse, the understanding of truth. You darken these things with your evil. Your passion for getting what you want consumes all, like destructive fire. The blood seeps out, because the acts of kindness that you've done were for your own evil purposes, and so you've misused these actions, and done violence to them."

Bardaric glared at the scepter with fear and anger. "That thing from the Mountains...," he muttered.

"It reveals the truth," Brandun testified, "because it comes from a place where the truth is revealed."

"Did you know, Brandun, that that is what 'Jahaziel' means?" Aeldra interjected, her voice shaky.

Brandun turned toward her.

"It means 'God reveals.' Eadric asked, and was told that in the Mountains."

Brandun smiled at her, and she managed to smile back.

Lord Bardaric was circling widely around the smoldering scepter. His eyes were menacing as he silently made his way back toward the bed. Brandun dashed in the other direction, around the bed and toward the door.

"No!" Bardaric objected, angry desperation in his voice.

But Brandun was already pulling open the heavy wooden door. "Help!" he cried out. "Come in at once!"

The two guards stepped in cautiously, overcome with confusion. "How did you get in here?" asked one. "Lord Bardaric, Queen Aeldra, forgive us. I don't understand how...."

"He's an evil man," Brandun interrupted, pointing at Bardaric, "trying to take control of the kingdom with dark magic."

Running footsteps pounded up the hall, and Ladroc and Kempe burst in, followed by Defena and two other guards, familiar to Brandun — ones who had served Eadric. Kempe rushed to Brandun and clasped his shoulders.

"I wanted to follow you through the window when Ladroc told me," he said breathlessly. "But Ladroc thought we ought to wait a bit and see what happened."

"Your majesty," Ladroc said to the queen, "shall we take Lord Bardaric into custody?"

Bardaric shook his head. "Such accusations," he exclaimed, his voice back to its calm, silken tone. He approached the queen. "I cared for you, Aeldra," he appealed to her, softening his voice, "when your heart was broken."

Aeldra refused to look at him. "You didn't do it for me," she told him. "You did it for yourself. I felt something was wrong all along, but you confused me so...."

223

"He controlled your mind," Brandun assured her, "with magical arts. You couldn't help your confusion."

Aeldra nodded sadly, still looking down. "I've been weak. I miss Eadric so. I need him...." Her voice broke, and large tears spilled from her eyes. Brandun ran to her and sat on the edge of the bed.

"You must give the order for his arrest," he coaxed.

Aeldra looked up, finally meeting Bardaric's eyes. "The scepter confirms the truth," she said, then turned to the waiting guards and ordered, "Arrest this man for treason!"

Bardaric gazed at her with hatred. "Foolish, ungrateful woman," he said bitterly as the two guards that had come with Ladroc took his arms and led him out of the room.

Ladroc, Kempe and Defena gathered around the black, burning scepter in its pool of blood, staring in astonishment. Carefully, Brandun approached it, crouched down, and put his hand out. The fire dwindled, and the blood faded away. Then the young prince took the dark scepter in his hand and held it up. In a rush, the scepter restored itself to gold, dispelling the blackness, shining more brilliantly than ever.

Chapter 28

When Brandun told Ladroc all that had happened in the queen's bedchamber, the steward's eyes widened, and he nodded fervently.

"That was indeed black magic," he confirmed. "I've read of such things, though I never knew anyone who practiced it. It's a method of enslaving a person's mind, first by the sorcerer linking his thoughts with those of his victim, then seizing the mind, filling it only with the thoughts that the sorcerer wants to inflict. And the controlling of the breath! The long ago sorcerers knew that the lungs and the breathing are linked to a person's thinking. But King Daegmund outlawed such evil magic when he established the kingdom of Haefen. I always knew Bardaric was evil, but I didn't realize the extent of it."

The next few days were spent having Brandun and Kempe fully tell the tales of their journey. Aeldra cried when she heard of the dream visits with Eadric, shedding tears that she couldn't have while under Bardaric's control. Defena took a while to adjust to the news that Brandun would be king, and not Kempe. But she warmed to the idea gradually when she witnessed

225

Kempe's enthusiasm as he arranged to apprentice under Eadric's captain of the guard, and when Brandun assured her of his pledge to always honor Kempe's decisions in times of battle or rescue.

A messenger Brandun sent to Tamtun returned with a message from Lufu. "All is well and active in Tamtun," the messenger relayed. "The woman Lufu sends her warmest regards, and invites you to come pick herbs with her whenever you like. She also sent you this," he concluded, and emptied a tiny cloth bag into Brandun's palm. A round bulb of garlic rolled out, and Brandun burst out laughing as he clutched it.

Shyly, Brandun came around to talking about Larke, and requested that she and her family attend the ceremony that would announce him as heir. Aeldra raised her eyebrows at first that Brandun had chosen a commoner to be his wife, but when she listened to Brandun describe her, her face softened, and she smiled warmly.

"You know it is usual for those of noble birth to marry other nobles, and to have had those marriages arranged by their parents. But Eadric and I were allowed to have a say in the matter of our marriage, so we wanted to allow you and Kempe to choose. It sounds as if this Larke has many noble qualities. If you care for her, I am happy."

Brandun reddened. At almost fourteen, he still felt young to be talking about marriage. In Haefen, it was not unusual to have girls marry at fourteen or fifteen, but young men tended to wait until sixteen or older. When he thought about Larke, there was a comfortable, happy feeling he had never experienced before, and a longing to see her. What was it supposed to feel like, wanting to marry someone?

Three weeks later, Brandun sat on a bench, leaning forward on the stone sill of his bedroom window. Below, he could see the crowds gathering in the courtyard for Aeldra's announcement, proclaiming him the heir. He sighed. He was glad to be home and back with Aeldra and Ladroc, but there was still a heaviness in the castle without Eadric's presence.

You would be amazed how close I stay to you, Eadric had said. If only he could see him. There seemed so many things one had to believe without seeing.

Make an effort to notice, a thought said to him. Yes, that was it, thought Brandun, sitting up. When he had made the effort, he had sensed the Light in himself, and in the good people in Larke's village. Perhaps he could find ways to sense Eadric with him, when he was learning how to be a good king. Any joy he felt in ruling or learning to rule was something Eadric could share with him.

And there was the future. He thought anxiously and excitedly about Larke's arrival. It was a week's journey from her village to the castle. Would she make it in time for the ceremony? And again, what could he say to her? There was still the unanswered question of a future marriage between them.

"Brandun," a voice called. Brandun turned to see Kempe standing in the doorway, dressed in regal clothing similar to his own. "I have a message for you — from Larke."

Brandun's heart leaped, and his face must have shown it, because Kempe laughed.

"I was in the courtyard, fetching my sword from the polisher, and just as I turned to enter the keep again, a travel-worn family came clattering over the drawbridge, two piled on each horse, and I heard Larke call my name."

He paused, and Brandun grabbed his arm, shaking it in exasperation. "And?" he demanded.

Kempe laughed again. "They had to head right into the crowd so as not to miss the ceremony, but she wanted to send you a message immediately."

Brandun thought he would burst, but held his tongue.

"She said, awkwardly, quite embarrassed, that she would be honored to be betrothed to you, and to spend her life married to such a good friend."

Brandun grinned, a grin that almost split his face. "And who will *you* marry, Kempe," he asked, shoving his cousin good-naturedly. "Why, you're already sixteen!"

"Never mind. I'll find her," Kempe retorted with a smile. "Now that I'm feeling happier with life, I may begin to look. But come. I was also supposed to tell you that it's time to go out on the balcony."

Brandun reached for the scepter which lay on a bench beside him. Smoothing out his tunic of red velvet and satin, he walked to the doorway, then habitually reached up to smooth his hair. Laughing, Kempe reached out and vigorously rumpled his younger cousin's curls.

"It's time you learned to accept those curls," he said lightly. "They're really quite handsome." Kempe threw a friendly arm around Brandun's shoulder, and together they left the bedroom, Brandun trying to comb his hair back into some sort of order with his fingers.

They passed through Eadric and Aeldra's bedroom chamber, and out to another hallway that led to the east side of the keep. Walking through open doors they stepped onto a balcony which overlooked the courtyard. There, Aeldra was addressing her subjects.

"After journeying to the Jahaziel Mountains," she announced, "after much travel and acts of bravery, and much searching for truth, the nephews of King Eadric of the golden eagle reached the Temple of Wisdom, and returned to tell us their news. I present to you first, the future captain of our armed forces, and right hand man to the king, Prince Kempe, son of Cadaham!"

A mighty cheer went up, and Kempe walked onto the balcony, waving to the people, his auburn hair looking almost golden in the midday sun. Brandun felt pride and gratitude at having gained such a friend.

"And now," Aeldra continued, "I present to the citizens of Haefen, the heir to the throne and the next king of this land, Prince Brandun of the golden horse, son of Regenfrith!"

Another cheer exploded from the crowd, and Brandun walked out to the balcony railing, watching the sea of color and movement spread out below him, feeling the power and support of the people. A hand was laid on his right shoulder. He turned to look into Kempe's smiling face and grinned. Aeldra took his left hand and squeezed it affectionately, and he clasped hers as well.

Looking again at the cheering crowd, Brandun felt peaceful knowing that he did not yet have to know how to care for them and solve all their problems. He would learn, bit by bit, and keep on learning forever. Up here were people who would help him learn. Down there somewhere was a girl who would stand beside him.

He raised his scepter high, drawing strength and confidence from his feelings of love, for his friends and his family, both those in this world and those in the life to come. Looking up at the wide expanse of blue sky, with its endless room to grow, he spoke in his mind to the loving, warm Light he had come to know in the Mountains.

Please, he prayed. *Keep me forever growing in wisdom.*

ACKNOWLEDGEMENTS

Of course, my main thanks goes to God. Without Him, I can do nothing. But there were many people that He used to help me.

Thanks to Anne Lambrix and the Institute of Children's Literature for assisting me in the writing of this book.

Thank you Donnette (Mom) for your financial and moral support. Thank you Daniel Eller and Karen Elder for all your work on the cover design. Thank you Nathan Odhner, Johanan Odhner, and Anjuli Elder for posing for the cover picture. Thank you Lisa Eller for the set up of the text. Thank you Garry Childs, Alan Elder, Bryn Brock, Cammie Manino, and Carol Buss for reading the story and giving me feedback. Thank you Gail Simons for editing, and Craig and Sarah McCardell for proofreading.

Thanks to my wonderful husband, Jon, for all the many ways he has helped and supported me to make this book a reality.

The scenes in the Jahaziel Mountains were inspired by descriptions in *True Christian Religion* by Emanuel Swedenborg.

ABOUT THE AUTHOR

Karin Alfelt Childs lives in Rochester, Michigan with her husband, Jon, and three of their children, Curtis, Bethany, and Matthew. Their oldest daughter, Annica, went into the "world beyond death" in 1991 after dying in a car accident when she was eight years old.